NIARA

By elizabeth griffin gore

Gore Publications
P. O. Box 43561
Philadelphia, PA 19106-3561

THANK YOU GOD FOR MAKING IT POSSIBLE

Published 1996 by:

Gore Publications
P. O. Box 43561
Philadelphia, PA 19106-3561

Library of Congress Cataloging-in-Publication Data
Griffin-Gore, Elizabeth
TXu 704-098

Fiction. I. Title

Cover airbrushed by: Smack 5
DEF. ART PRODUCTIONS
main office/ studio (215) 339-9413
Philadelphia, PA

Special Thanks to Ahmed Tahir
Pearl of Africa
(215) 413-8995
624 South Street
Philadelphia, PA 19147

Printed in Canada

ZOO TIME

RED BALLOONS FLOATING HIGH

UP UP UP INTO A CLEAR **BLUE** SKY

VISIONS OF ZOO IN MY EYE

ANIMALS LAUGHING

GORILLAS GRASPING

AS I WALK BY

ELEPHANTS BLOWING THEIR

TRUNKS SO LOUD

AS THEY GAZE INTO THE CROWD

GIRAFFES GRAZING ABOVE MY

HEAD

LIONS LAZING ON A GREAT BIG **BED**

LOVE, JARIN ERIN ERIC DERRICK

Much Appreciation To The Following Book Stores
Afro-Missions
Arnim
Rhoda
Hayden
Basic Black Books/Philadelphia, PA
(215) 922-4417
Lccia
Sheila
Hakim's/ Philadelphia, PA
(215) 474-9495
Angela
Glenda
Haneef's Bookstore/Wilmington, DE
(302) 656-4193
Haneef
LaUnique/ Camden, NJ
(856) 338-1958
Larry
Liguorius/Philadelphia, PA
(215) 886-3675
Betty
Pearl of Africa/Philadelpia, PA
(215) 413-8995
Ahmed
Norman
Robin's Bookstore/Philadelphia, PA
(215) 735-9600
Larry
It's A Mystery To Me/Yeadon, PA
(610) 623-1006
Juanita

4

ACKNOWLEDGEMENT

I want to truly thank all the people who have supported me and helped me to dream my dreams...

Daddy
Aunt Lucille
Uncle David
David C. Griffin
Walter P. Griffin
Angel Lee Hicks
Nancy Gore
David Gore
Lisa Jones
Antwyne Jones
Terri Griffith
Ronald Griffith
Aleshia Patterson
James Patterson-- Scooter
Lashante Vorters
D. W. G.
Pamela Perry
Ramona Rider

Miss Jessie Mae Coleman
Shelby Coleman
Dorothy Coleman
Rebecca Coleman
Amelia Coleman
Jenita Coleman
Wanda Gilbert
Diane Douglass
Brenda Douglass
The Douglass Family
Diana Nobles
Jacqueline Waters
Terry Medford

5

McDonald's Crew at 13th and Market
Mrs. Elnora Felder
Marietta Brown
Anthony Grier
Jenell
Michael
Mervis
Ron
Bessie
Richard
Solomon
Jessie
George
Albert
Anne
Sarah
Vanessa
Gaylicnca
Lois
Leela
Beatrice
Lurie
Merci
Martha
Thelma
Elaine
Peggy
Tracy
Sylvia
Caryn Lennon
Chemistry Lab
Hematology Lab
Environmental Services
Roy Graham
April Whitehead
Ziggy
James
Robert
Charles

to

black girls

asian girls

SPANISH GIRLS

native american girls

indian girls

african girls

all girls

don't let the height of your skirt
or
the fit of your clothes
or
the length of your hair
or
the size of your butt
or
the cuteness of your face
or
the complexion of your skin
or
the color of your eyes
or
the jewelry you wear
define who you are
let it be the brain you possess
and what you put into it

7

PREFACE

"I'm not gonna make it."

I struggled to get into the elevator. My arms were wrapped around my enormous belly. I felt a tightening sensation at the base of it-- like someone with big hands was squeezing me there and then suddenly releasing me.

"You gotta try girl. You can't have it here."

"I know-- but I can't walk."

I was panting heavier than before. I had no control over my breathing; it was erratic.

"Come on. You gotta."

"I can't-- "

I tried to continue speaking, but I had to stop. I could feel the pain coming. Tears ran down my face as I anticipated it. The pain wasn't like any I had experienced before-- not like cramps, or a toothache, or even a sucker punch. And there was nothing I could do to lessen it. It came and went when it wanted to. I was helpless to stop it.

Somehow I managed to get inside the elevator. I forced myself to walk. I had no choice.

"What floor?" asked Lisa.

"Five," I said not even bothering to look up at her. I was trying to block her and the pain out, but that didn't work. I felt another contraction beginning.

"I can't believe you was gonna come here all by yourself.

9

Where is your Mom?"

"I don't know--" I stopped speaking; I had to. The pain gripped me in the stomach and caused me to double-over and groan. It eventually passed and I was able to continue speaking.

"I guess she's with one of her men friends. I woke up this morning and she wasn't there. Some of her stuff was gone too."

"She's with some man?" disbelief was all over Lisa's face.

"It won't be the first time."

"That's not right. Can't you find her?"

"What for?"

"She should be here. She knew you was gonna have this baby soon."

"Forget her Lisa. She wasn't around no other time. Why should now be different--"

Another contraction was coming. I braced myself for it, but the pain was more severe this time. I opened my mouth and groaned loudly, "Ahhhooouu!" I did this until it subsided. Lisa could do nothing but watch.

We stepped from the elevator and looked around. There was a sign on the wall directing us to the labor and delivery room.

"Did your water break?"

"I don't think so."

I was so glad I ran into Lisa on my way here. She was getting off the thirteen trolley when I spotted her. I was waiting on the other side of the street for the one that would take me into the city. Now I would not have this baby all by myself.

"I wish Nathaniel was here."

"Cathleen please! Don't even think about him now. If he doesn't come, that's on him. It's his loss."

10

"I called-- and left a message with his roommate. Do you think he might change his mind about the baby? I mean after it gets here--"

"I doubt it girl. You might as well start moving on with your life and forget him."

"He could change his mind."

"Yeah right, and I'm not really black either," said Lisa sarcastically.

"I hope I have a boy. You think he might come if it's a boy? I could name him Nathaniel."

"Don't you name that baby after him! He don't want to be a daddy. So naming your baby Nat ain't gonna do nothing. It won't make him come here tonight."

"He might," I panted out. My words got caught in my throat as another pain came.

"Give it up Cathleen. He ain't here and he ain't coming. Just be glad his mother accepts you and the baby."

"Mrs. James has-- been real nice. She said she'd talk to him about the baby."

"It's not gonna do no good," said Lisa. "She'll be wastin' her time."

We struggled to the closed double doors, or rather Lisa dragged me to them. The doors had no windows. Just a sign telling us to push the silver pad on the side of the wall. We did that. The doors automatically opened. Inside I saw a bunch of nurses sitting together, some were using computers, others were just talking. As I looked on, one got up and walked toward us.

"Can I help you?" she asked briskly, examining my stomach with her eyes. Did I see disdain in them? Was she

11

judging me because I was young, and pregnant? Or was she simply tired of seeing girls destroying their futures at the ages of eleven, twelve, thirteen... Could that be why this nurse appeared to be callous.

"I think I'm about to have it," I said pointing to my stomach.

"Who is your doctor?"

"I'm from the clinic across the street. I don't know who my doctor is," I mumbled. "I mean I don't know who's on call tonight--"

The nurse interrupted me, "How many weeks are you?"

"Thirty-nine."

"Are you in labor?"

"I think so."

"Don't you know?" she scolded.

"Yeah I am."

"How fast are the contractions coming?"

"I don't know."

"When is your due date?"

"February 10th."

"Your name?" she asked.

"Cathleen Saunders."

"I'll see if I can locate your file," she said and then walked away.

The nurse stopped in front of the metal cabinet on wheels. She bent down and ran her fingers across the red binders as she read the names quickly.

As she continued looking she spoke, "I do not see it. If you are due next week, it should be here. Could you be at the wrong hospital?" she asked accusingly.

"No I'm not. I've been going to the clinic across the street ever since I got pregnant."

"Well your file is not here. Are you sure about your due date?"

"Don't she look like she's about to have a baby?" jumped in Lisa.

"I have had people get hospitals and dates confused," the nurse replied. "I've spent a lot of time in the past looking for files on people who should have gone to the hospital on tenth street instead of here."

"It's the right hospital," I said.

"Well maybe someone forgot to send your file over," the nurse said in an agitated voice. "Why can't people ever do things right?" she said giving no indication of who she was talking about.

"I got to sit down-- I can't stand anymore," I said bending over further. "I feel pressure down there," I pointed to the bottom of my stomach.

"Can she sit?" asked Lisa.

"As soon as I find out who her doctor is."

"But she needs a room? She can't stand here forever."

"In a minute. Housekeeping is cleaning it," she said picking up a phone and dialing. She talked into the receiver for several minutes then she hung it up and came back to us.

"One of the clinic doctors is on his way here," she informed me.

"Thanks," I said automatically. I didn't mean it; it was simply a conditioned response.

"Are you a family member?" I heard the nurse ask Lisa.

13

"I'm her girlfriend-- do you have a problem with that?"

"No I do not. But I am her nurse for tonight, and I do not need any additional problems to complicate my job."

"I ain't no problem," said Lisa.

"Good."

The nurse walked away again without saying a word. She picked up a clipboard and began writing on it.

"She is rude," declared Lisa. "What is she doing?"

"I don't know, but here she comes again."

"Come on," the nurse said, leading us into a corner. She walked fast and we followed her as best we could. In the corner was a curtained off room. It contained a slanted table with two metal objects attached to the end of it. White paper covered the table and there was a pillow lying on it.

"Can I get something for this pain?"

"No. What number baby will this make?" asked the nurse.

"But it hurts-- so bad."

"Her first," answered Lisa.

"Thank you but, I need Cathleen to answer these questions."

I could tell Lisa didn't like what the nurse said. She was getting upset, but she didn't say another word.

"Any abortions?"

"No."

"Any complications during pregnancy?"

"No."

"What is your date of birth?"

"November 5th 1969."

"Any problems with medications?"

14

"No."

I watched the nurse check off several other things on her clipboard before she handed it to me, "You must sign this consent form before we can deliver your baby."

"I already signed one."

"It's across the street. And that's not going to help us right now."

I took the board and signed it.

"Get undressed and put this on," she said tossing me a gown. "And give me a urine sample. Void some into the toilet then collect the rest in this container," she said resting it on the bed.

"Void?"

"Pee into the toilet and then put the rest into that container-- do you understand?"

"Yeah," I said.

"Why do you want that?" asked Lisa. "Are you checking her for drugs?"

"I want to check for protein-- why? Should I be looking for drugs also?"

"I don't do nothing," I said.

"If that were true, you wouldn't be here," she said and walked out of the room.

"No she didn't say that. I know she didn't even tell you that," ranted Lisa. "Who the hell does she think she is? She needs to be doing her job instead of getting all in your business," she said walking to the edge of the room and announcing it loudly.

"Don't worry about her," I said.

"But, I don't like her Cathleen."

"Neither do I, but I don't really care about her right now. This pain is getting worser," I said removing my clothes. "I'm gonna tell that nurse I need something real bad."

"She's not gonna give you nothing. You'll have to wait for the doctor."

"How do you know that?"

"'cause that's how they did my sister."

"Well he betta hurry up and get here. I can't take much more of this."

"I know," said Lisa walking up behind me. "I'll tie that for you."

I felt her cold hands and fingers touching my neck as she knotted the strings on my gown. "Your butt looks damn ashy," she said laughingly. "The doctor's gonna see that and tell you to go home and put some lotion on."

"I don't look that bad, do I?"

"No," she teased.

"Even if I did, I ain't going no place, but to the bathroom," I said picking up the plastic container.

The nurse didn't tell me where the bathroom was. Nor did she pull the curtains shut or even tell us her name. I hadn't realized that before.

"Nurse!" yelled Lisa. "Where is the bathroom?"

"Straight back and to your left," she answered from the nurse's station.

"I bet she's lying about the pee. She's probably checking you for drugs. I bet they do that to all the black girls that come in here."

"Well she won't find nothing on me."

16

"I know that, but they're still gonna test you. Do you want me to go with you?"

"I can do it by myself."

"Are you sure?"

"Yeah. Unless you are going to pee in this thing for me," I teased.

"Nah. I can't do that. Then it might come up positive for something."

"Girl you need to stop that. I know you ain't-- doing nothing either," I said wishing this baby would hurry up and come.

"Try telling them that," she said pointing to the nurses. "I know they're talking about us."

Lisa was sixteen too, but she had no kids. She wasn't trying to have any either. I know she goes out with a lot of different boys, but that was it. She said she wasn't giving up the butt, and so far I guess she hadn't. She wasn't like me. She had decided way back that she would not be one of them girls in the neighborhood who got pregnant. She wasn't about having babies; she liked her freedom too much. She was forever saying, 'I ain't got time for no babies. Once you have them, you don't have time for nothing else-- look at my mother.'

I do not know how many steps I took before I felt this hot liquid splashing against my inner thighs, ankles and feet. My sneakers absorbed a lot of it, but the liquid kept coming. It formed a puddle around me and then gradually traveled off into different directions.

"I'm bleeding!" I screamed afraid to look down. "It won't stop!"

I stood rigid; I was afraid to move any part of my body just

17

in case my baby wanted to follow the path the blood took. I heard Lisa yelling for the nurse.

"She needs help!" Lisa called out. She was the first to reach me.

"It's not blood Cat. Your water broke."

"It did?" I said looking down at it.

"Come on girl. I'll get you back to the room."

"I can't move. What if the baby is coming?" I asked not budging.

"Then you shouldn't be standing here. Come on."

Obeying Lisa, I took slow, unsure steps. Why wasn't the nurse doing this? Where was she anyway? I thought her job was to help me.

No sooner had I thought those questions than the nurse ran up to my free arm and helped me into another room. It was unfamiliar. It looked extremely sterile and bright. There was a massive light hovering over a crisp white bed. Its sheets were folded back and very uninviting. I wanted to question the change in rooms, but the pain reduced my need to know to a slight curiosity. I allowed them to help me into the bed.

"I-- can't take this-- please give me something-- anything," sweat was suddenly rolling down my face and into my eyes and mouth.

"I cannot do that. The doctor is the only person who can give you meds. Lift up. I need to put this around your waist."

I did as she asked. She slid a thick belt underneath me. She then squirted a cold gel onto my stomach. I grimaced; it felt like jello. The nurse smeared the gooey stuff all over my stomach and then fastened the belt around my waist. She pulled it so tight I thought the baby was going to look chinese. And then, she slid a cold, black device beneath the belt.

"What's that for?" I barely got the words out. The belt was extremely tight.

"To monitor the baby's heart rate."

I listened to the monitor. I wanted to say the baby sounded like it was under water every time I heard the heart beat, but I held the words back. I didn't want to appear dumb.

I looked away from the belt around my waist, and watched the nurse studying the lined paper coming from a machine. On the continuous sheet of paper, a needle scribbled exaggerated triangles.

"Your contractions are very close--" her speaking was interrupted by a tall black man walking into the room. He looked African. I don't mean African-American. I mean African-African. And I could tell by Lisa's face, she thought he was cute.

"Hello Cathleen," he said with a thin, barely noticeable accent. When he pronounced my name, he stressed the first syllable and allowed the last one to glide past his lips rather quickly. "How are you doing?"

"Can I get something for the pain?"

"After I examine you," he gave me a slight smile. "I must see how far along you are. I am Dr. Adom."

I smiled right back at him. I could see the nurse's whole attitude change up when he walked in. I liked his affect on her.

"Has her blood work been drawn?"

"I was about to do a complete blood count."

"Draw a type and screen also, but hold it. We might not need it."

Picking up all the things she needed to draw my blood, the

19

nurse approached me. She dumped her supplies on the bed beside me. I watched her attach a needle to something yellow. She then tied a long rubbery tube tightly around my arm.

"Pump your fist like this," she said showing me what to do.

"Okay," I said pumping.

"You can stop now."

She punctured my skin and filled two tubes with my blood. I watched her discard the needle when she was finished. She wrote my name on the tubes and put one into a plastic bag with a long green and white slip. The other tube she stuck into a rack.

Dr. Adom stood in the background as the nurse got the blood. Once she was finished, he stepped forward again.

"I want to check your cervix," he said. "Move down on the bed. I want you to put your feet into the stirrups. Nurse do we have large gloves in here?"

"Right here," she said handing him the box.

"Thank you," he said slipping the latex gloves on.

The nurse threw a sheet over my stomach. I couldn't see too much of anything now.

"You are going to feel pressure," he said forcing his hand into my vagina and up the birth canal.

"Arrrhhhh!" I screamed, screwing up my face.

"I know this is not comfortable," he said forcing his hand even further toward my cervix. "But I must see how many centimeters you have dilated. You are doing good," he encouraged.

He straightened from his bending position in front of me and removed his soiled gloves. "Eight centimeters. You are going to be there soon."

20

"Can I please get something? I can't take this anymore."

"You do not need heavy anesthesia now. Your labor is progressing well. And it is better for the baby. I will have the nurse put 7.5 cc of Demerol into your I.V."

"Oh no! Here comes another one!" I screamed closing my eyes.

"Do not close your eyes," Dr. Adom commanded. "Focus on the clock."

I looked at him. Then at the clock.

"Good. You are doing good Cathleen. Take a deep breath. Hold it. Now count."

"I can't," I burst out. "Oh god it-- it hurts so bad."

"Yes you can do it. The contraction will be over soon. Take another deep breath. Slowly, come on-- count to ten."

I took the air into my mouth. One-- two-- three-- four-- five. That was as far as I got. The contraction ended."

"Nurse get that I.V. into her before the next contraction."

"Yes Dr. Adom."

"I feel it coming again," I said hysterically. "I can't do this--"

"The nurse is going to give you something to dull the pain."

All I could think of when he said that was, not another needle. Wasn't I in enough pain?

I was barely aware of the nurse working on me. I was too obsessed with the pain gripping my lower belly.

Dr. Adom turned to Lisa and said, "You hold her hand and make sure she focuses on that clock when the next contraction starts."

"Me? I don't know nothing about having a baby!" she

exclaimed.

"It does not matter. You can still help. Look at that paper," he said pointing to the paper attached to a machine. "When the line on that paper begins climbing up, she will be starting a contraction-- like this one here," he pointed to a jagged triangle. "When it goes down, the contraction will be ending. Have her take deep breaths when each contraction begins. Tell her to relax when it is over."

"I'll try," said Lisa.

"Aurrghh-- it's coming!"

"Stop talking Cathleen. Look at the clock," Dr. Adom directed.

"I can't take this pain!"

He then looked at Lisa, "You are her coach now."

"Cat count-- come on. One, two, three," instructed Lisa.

"I can't--"

"Yes you can."

"Okay, okay," I panted. "I'll try."

"Take a big breath. Hold it. Now come on, count."

"I'm counting. I'm counting."

"No you're not."

"One," I was panting heavily. "Two, three, four..."

"That's it. Now you are counting. Good," said Lisa.

"You can relax," said Dr. Adom. "It has ended."

I laid drenched on the bed. Sweat was covering me from head to foot. My hospital gown clung to me. I laid in this state until I saw the nurse approaching me. Apprehension was displayed on my face. She had a clear plastic bag full of some kind of liquid. What was she going to do with that? I watched her hang the bag

22

on a metal pole.

"I am going to hook you up to this I.V. It will make the contractions less severe."

"Okay," I mumbled through dry, white lips.

I winced when I felt the needle being inserted into the top side of my wrist. I immediately felt a coolness flowing through my veins. I was getting cold. I pulled the blankets up to my chin, and tried to relax a little.

The next forty minutes took a long time to pass. But somewhere between all the screaming and hollering, I noticed Dr. Adom pulling on another pair of gloves.

"I am going to check your cervix again," he said. "Move down to the end of the table ."

"Not again!"

"I must continue to do this until you reach ten centimeters. You're getting there."

He checked me. This time I was nine and a half centimeters. He assured me that I was almost there. Almost was not good enough. When was I going to be ten centimeters? When was he going to tell me to push like they did in all the movies?

I laid on the bed completely quiet except for when the contractions peaked. Then I was a wild person thrashing all over the place and begging them to give me something stronger to stop the pain.

Lisa continued to feed me ice chips when I complained I was thirsty, but that didn't help..

When was he going to tell me to push? When was this going to end?

After examining my cervix two more painful times, Dr.

Adom finally said what I wanted to hear, "I do not feel your cervixes Cathleen. When the next contraction begins, I want you to push."

Push? Was I finally going to be able to do that? All night long I had been told not to push and now six hours later I was going to be allowed to push. My legs were being held apart and everyone was chanting for me to push.

I tucked my chin deep into my chest, clenched my teeth together and pushed with the concentration of a desperate person. It was a long push that quickly ran out of energy.

"Can I stop?" I asked out of breath. My hair was sticking to my head. Sweat was everywhere.

"The contraction is over. You can stop," the nurse said.

I laid there catching my breath, hoping the next wave of pain would take a break. But that was not going to be. I felt the building of tense sensations and I knew the next one was coming.

"Another contraction is here," Dr. Adom announced looking at the graphed paper. "Begin taking a deep breath."

"All right," I whispered.

When the contraction started, I pushed. My rectum exploded releasing everything it previously held. I could see the nurse wiping me down with disposable paper wipes.

"Push harder," the doctor demanded.

"I-- I'm trying," I said losing my energy again.

"You can relax. The contraction is finished," he said.

He told me to relax, but as soon as I did that the next contraction started mounting. How long was this going to last? I can't keep pushing like this. Especially without any drugs.

"I feel it again," I said warning them.

"Start pushing," he directed me.

"I am! I am!" I yelled.

"Push girl, come on," chanted Lisa along with the nurse and Dr. Adom.

"I can see the head," he said.

"Is it a boy?" I asked prematurely. The baby wasn't even born yet so how could he know the sex of it.

"Keep pushing."

The contractions were coming closer and closer together. And the pushing was progressing in the same fashion. I did not have much rest time in between the pains.

"All I need is a few more strong pushes Cathleen and it will be over. The head is almost out," said Dr. Adom.

"I'm trying-- Arrrrhhghh!" I screamed. I could feel my vagina being split apart by the pressure of the baby's head. It was like being sliced open by lightening.

"Get it outta me! Please-- get it out! It's killing me!"

In the midst of all the screaming and pain, I heard the doctor ordering me to, "Stop!"

Stop? Stop what? Pushing? Was he crazy? The baby was finally coming out and he wanted me to stop everything? He wanted me to not push anymore? Well, I couldn't just stop like that. I had waited too long for this moment. But what would happen if I didn't stop? Would I harm the baby? Would something happen to me? I was afraid to continue pushing. I felt my body trying to decide what to do next.

"We have to clear the baby's nose and throat," I heard Dr. Adom announce. It took them several seconds before the task was completed.

25

"Give me another push," he demanded.

"Arrrghh," I shrieked.

"Did you want a boy or a girl?" he asked.

"Yes," I whispered not realizing what I was saying.

"You have a daughter, Cathleen," he announced like a proud father would.

"I do?" was all I could say.

He laid her warm and slippery body onto my chest. The first thing I saw when he placed her there were these two big grayish eyes. They were not blinking. They just stared at me and I stared back into them. She was beautiful. I could see that even through her slimy purple face.

"She's a cutie," said Lisa standing next to me and peering into the little baby's face.

"She certainly is," said Dr. Adom, stroking the top of her head. Then he said in a soft and extremely serious voice, "I do not want to see you in my delivery room again until you are a woman. Do you hear me?"

I was startled by his words, but I said, "Yes."

"Good," he smiled. "And take care of my baby."

"I will."

I touched her check delicately, testing to see if she would allow me. When she did not resist, I slowly began to caress her incredibly soft cheek. I was content to do this until Dr. Adom insisted that I push one final time in order to get the placenta out.

As I obeyed him, the nurse took the baby from me. But, I followed her with my eyes. She put the baby into a glass crib and began examining her. I saw her put something into the baby's eyes. She was examining my baby's hands and mouth. She then

26

wrote something down onto a chart. She took the baby's temperature. She then put a diaper on her. "She was born at 5:05pm," the nurse said for my benefit. Seeing that she was fine, I closed my eyes and allowed the doctor to massage my uterus into place. I gritted my teeth and thanked God that is was over.

When I opened them again, it was to a quiet labor and delivery room. The baby was gone; Lisa was gone; the doctor was gone and so was the nurse. I checked myself underneath the blankets. My bleeding had stopped a great deal. I felt a little lightheaded though.

I got to get up! I got to call Nathaniel! Tell him about the baby-- that he's a father-- that he has a daughter!

I didn't know how, but somehow I had to get up and into a sitting position.

Struggling a bit, I finally managed to sit up. I rested for a moment. I felt a gush of blood down below. Was that normal? Was I supposed to bleed like that? I stopped and waited to see if it would happen again. It did not. I pulled the metal I.V. pole closer to the bed. I needed it to support my weight as I stood up. I made my way to my jeans hanging on a rack. Pulling out my change purse, I carefully and slowly walked to the pay phone in the waiting room. I dragged the I.V. pole with me.

The nurses were not paying attention to me so I had no problem getting to the phone. It was on the other side of the nurse's station.

Picking up the black receiver, I dialed his number. A recording spoke into my ear telling me to deposit a dollar and forty-five cents. I did exactly as she said. Then I heard a ringing sound. I counted six rings before someone picked up and a male voice spoke:

"Hello-- hello? Who is it?"

"It's me. Cathleen. I'm at the hospital."

He said nothing. There was no noise in his background. He simply waited for me to talk.

"I had it-- the baby. It's a girl."

"Why do you keep calling me?" he said in a chilling voice.

"I thought you'd want to know when I had it. It's your baby too--"

"Says you."

"It is," I insisted.

"Well I don't want to know nothing about no baby or you. If you was stupid enough to get pregnant, then that's your problem. Not mine."

"Why are you talking to me like that? I never did nothing to you."

"You haven't? You got my mother all in my business. Now she expects me to be some kind of father to it."

"But you should--"

"Don't you tell me what I should do. Not you. Some little 'ho from nowhere."

"I ain't no whore. You was my first."

"Yeah right and I'm supposed to believe that too? You knew what you was getting into."

"I thought you liked me--"

"Girl I ain't got time for this. You knew what I was about. And you was down with it too. So don't start pretending you wasn't."

NIARA

"I didn't just want sex--"

"I got two more years at this university and I ain't blowing it because of some summer thing. I've been going for too long to let some kid ruin everything for me."

"What about the baby?"

"What about it?"

"I can't take care of her by myself."

"Get on Welfare-- I don't care what you do, but don't look for me to help you."

"Are you gonna come see her?"

"Aren't you listening? I don't want to see her. She's not my concern."

"I-- haven't named her yet. You got any ideas?"

"No I don't! And stop calling me!" he said and then hung up the telephone.

I stood leaning against the phone with tears in my eyes. I could feel the blood running down my legs. When did I begin bleeding? I hadn't noticed it until now. I had to get back to my room! I took one step and thought I was going to fall down. I tried to take another step, but I stopped. I felt more blood rushing down my legs. Harsh cramps gripped my stomach. I had to hurry! A puddle had already formed on the floor. I felt dizzy...

CHAPTER ONE

"Why is she here?"

I asked the question of no one in particular as I watched the black woman lean into the casket. She was thin and dressed in dark gray. Her hair was drawn away from her face and coiled neatly into a black knot. The hairdressing suited her. It made her look cold which was how I expected her to be.

I could not see her eyes. But if I had, I would not have expected to see the tears that were present. And if I had seen them, I would've wondered how she could shed them so freely for a woman she hadn't seen in thirteen years. What emotions could she possibly be feeling? She was incapable of anything, but selfishness. I knew this from first hand experience.

The woman walked away from the alter after several minutes; and without much hesitation, she began moving towards us.

"I know she's not coming over here!" I said sarcastically. Disbelief was visible in my eyes.

"Who girl?" asked Grandfather.

"Cathleen."

"I don't see her-- where?"

"Over by the flower," I said, but as I spoke the woman advanced pass the arrangement and was approaching us.

Grandfather did not see Cathleen until she was up on him.

"George, I'm so sorry," said the woman.

"Thank you," he said standing up and moving into

the aisle. "We all knew it was going to happen. The cancer was just too much for her. It's better this way."

"I'm so sorry," she repeated.

He nodded his head in understanding.

"Why should you be sorry?" I asked in a quiet almost inaudible voice.

Cathleen gave me a surprised glance, but continued to address my Grandfather, " I had to come."

"Why?" I spoke louder this time.

"Niara!" he reprimanded.

"She's being a hypocrite."

"Your   grandmother has just died," he said.   "That's enough to be sorry for."

"It doesn't mean nothing to her-- nobody has seen her in years. Now she comes in here talking about she's sorry."

"Niara!" he said in a silencing voice. "That's your mother. Let her talk."

"Mother? What kind of mother is she? I haven't seen her since I was three. Why should I care what she has to say?"

"Because I am telling you to," said Grandfather. "Now close your mouth."

"But she shouldn't even be here," I said.

"What's your problem?" asked Cathleen.

"You," I said. "You're a joke. You come walking in here like you got rights. Nobody wants you here. Why don't you leave?"

"Be quiet Niara! You've said enough," said Grandfather. He then directed his next words to Cathleen, "I've been worried about you."

"I know," her words trailed off.

"I'm glad you called to tell me what happened."

"You should be here," said Grandfather.

"You called her!" I screamed.

"She's your mother, girl," he said lowering his voice. "You're going to need her now that Nancy's gone."

"For what? I don't need her or Nathaniel. I don't need none of them."

The man who was supposed to be my father was sitting away from us with his wife and children. I've only seen him three times in my whole life. He was a big joke too-- treating me like a stepchild. He never came to see me or even bothered to waste a quarter to call me.

"You're always going to need family," said Grandfather.

"Not her," I said.

"I don't want to argue with you Niara. Not here. We can work things out later," said the woman.

"There's nothing to work out!" I don't know when I stood up or how I became so loud. But I had to get away from her.

"Niara don't open your mouth again," said Grandfather. "Do you hear me?"

"But I don't want her here."

Cathleen spoke up, "Do you listen to you Grandfather?"

"Yes I listen to him."

"Don't seem like it. You're still talking."

"And you're still here."

"Niara! Be quiet!" said Grandfather harshly; his bloodshot eyes were looking at me. I could see thin veins covering the white parts of his eyes. He hadn't slept since Grandmother died. All he did was listen to the radio.

"Cathleen sit down. We can talk about everything else later."

"Sit down? What are you talking about? She can't do that. She can't sit here-- next to us. She's not family," I challenged.

"I think you should remember that you are only a child," she said in a loud voice. "And, I am family. I am your mother-- like it or not that's how it is. I'm the one that gave birth to you."

"Gave birth to me? What's that supposed to mean? You're the one who also gave me away. You aren't my family. You are nothing!"

"You know? You are one rude little girl. But you better watch your mouth , 'cause I can get just as nasty."

"You get what you deserve," I said.

"Sit down!" I heard someone from behind us whisper.

"I'm sorry," said Cathleen maneuvering pass Grandfather.

"But this isn't right!" I protested.

"She's here now Niara so move over and make room. I shouldn't have to tell you that again."

"But you're not really going to let her sit with us?" I repeated angrily.

"Yes he is. Move over," said Cathleen.

"No. I won't do it."

"You don't have a choice," said the thin woman.

"Then I'll move."

"Sit your butt down girl," she said grasping my arm and pulling me down into the space next to her.

"Don't you touch me," I said snatching my arm away from

her.

"Girl you're pushing it."

Cathleen glared at me. She was angry, but I think she was also a little surprised at how I was treating her. What did she expect? Did she think I'd be glad to see her? Here? At Grandmother's funeral? I hadn't seen her in over thirteen years She hadn't visited me once in all that time. Or tried to contact me. So she shouldn't really be surprised that I didn't want her here. I don't have a mother. The woman next to me was a stranger. Somebody I didn't know or even want to know.

"I can tell you one thing. I'm not going to tolerate this kind of talk in my house--" she stopped speaking abruptly and looked away quickly. She would not look at me.

"What? What did you say?"

"Nothing,"

"Yes you did," I continued to probe.

"Forget it."

"You wcrc going to say 'my housc' wcrcn't you?"

"Forget it." she said.

"That's what you meant-- didn't you?" I demanded.

"Now is not the time for this," said Cathleen.

"For what?" I asked looking at her. "What are you talking about?"

"I can't get into it right now. This is not the place."

"It's the only place you'll see me," I said sarcastically.

I then turned to my Grandfather, "What's she talking about Grandpah?"

"Later girl."

"Will somebody tell me something?" I said getting louder.

"Am I supposed to go to your house for a visit? Is that it? Is that what you are thinking? If that's it, you are wrong. You can forget it, because this is the last time I ever want to see you."

"It won't be for a visit Niara," she blurted out probably in an effort to hurt me. "You will be living with me," she said in a tone equally as mean as mine.

"You must be tripping," I said. "I live with Grandpah. Why should I suddenly go live with you? I don't even like you."

"Right now I feel the same way too," she said.

"That's fine with me, but you must be crazy or something if you think I'm staying with you. Why should I?"

"I'm trying not to get angry girl, but you are making it hard. You better watch who you are talking to."

"And if I don't? What are you going to do?"

"I'm going to make you regret--"

Before Cathleen could complete her response, Grandfather leaned over in our direction and simply said, "Allow me to say goodbye to my wife. Show her some respect Niara."

Then he turned to Cathleen, "Please hold off saying anything else."

"You're right George. I'm sorry. I've said too much already."

Hold off saying what? I didn't know what they had planned, but I was not going anywhere with her. I could barely stand being near her. So living with her was totally out. They could both forget it. I glanced in the direction of my father and his family. He was holding his baby in his lap. As I stared at him, I could not help but hate him too. How could he be a father to them and not be one to me? What did I do that he could hate me

35

for so long? It was not my fault he didn't want me. I had no control over any of that. So I hated him.

I looked again at the woman seated next to me. How could she just give me away? What reason did she have? I forced my brain to remember-- to go back to when I was three. I strained and strained until I began to remember something...

The memories were sluggish almost refusing to come alive again after so many years of disuse. But they did come back. They were the product of what had been told to me by my grandmother, what I vaguely remembered on my own and my subconscious. I began to remember my mother's voice yelling at me. I was standing in the doorway of her bedroom; my eyes locked on her tall, slim frame. My ears listening to her every word. The words she spoke were harsh-- uncaring, but I was too young to realize it.

'WHY DID I EVEN BOTHER HAVING YOU?' *I heard my mother say..."I should've gotten an abortion instead of having that nigger's baby. It's my own fault, though. It was me who said yes and let him do it to me. I should've known he didn't really want me. All he wanted was some sex. Now look at me, I'm stuck with you!" I said, staring at Niara.*

"I'm tired of living like this. I got no money for nothing-- I'm the one who's always looking like some damn bum. Look at my hair," I said louder, startling my daughter. "It ain't been done in months. I'm surprised it's not falling out. And my nails look bad as hell. I never used to look like this."

I walked over to the bedroom window and looked out. The street below was busy with people going on with their lives. Ms. Griffin was waiting on the bus with her four children.

Cynthia, the nineteen-year-old girl from down the street was carrying her pregnant butt to the corner laundry mat. She was pushing a cart full of dirty clothes. Her two dirty children ages two and three were running ahead of her; they weren't paying any attention to anybody but themselves.

I saw a girl sitting on the steps across the street from my apartment building. It was Paulette. She was fifteen and kind of pretty. She was talking to some boy. I shook my head. I guess it would just be a matter of time before he or some other boy got her pregnant too.

I didn't mean to raise the peeling window frame or even stick my head out of it, but that's what I did. All the hatred I felt for every black man who tread his muddy, stinking feet through my life came out in that instance. This included my father who helped me to become what I am-- a black bastard; my uncles who encouraged him to be that way, my brothers who didn't have time to love me, and all the other men who came into my life after Nathaniel. I hated them all!

"Get the hell away from her! She don't want no babies by you!" I screamed out.

The young couple on the steps jerked their heads up in uncoordinated unison. The girl appeared embarrassed as though I had overheard his sweet, empty promises. The pledges she would believe for a time until she discovered them to be as worthless as all his, 'I love yous.'

The boy reacted differently. He was agitated by my outburst, "Speak on what you know! I'm nothing like the guy who got your dumb butt pregnant-- so close the window and go back to your pathetic life."

"Yeah my life is that way, but so will hers be if she gets knocked up by you," I slammed down the window "Now think about that!"

I walked away. I didn't accomplish a thing. To them I was probably just some bitter, lonely nut. At least I tried to warn her which was more than I got.

I've been living here in West Philly for three years-- every since Niara was born. I hated it, but I couldn't live any better with the money I was getting from Welfare. I hated that too. I also hated being black and being poor. To me being black meant the same thing as being poor.

37

NIARA

I lived with two other girls just like me. They were also poor, black and on Welfare. Our checks all went to different addresses so that we would have no problem collecting them, but we lived together in an attempt to keep some of the money for ourselves. I wanted to start saving for a house; I wanted a place to raise Niara, but it was not working out because sometimes the other girls would leave their children on me and disappear for days. Or both the mothers and the children would leave when rent was due and come back afterwards with some sorry story. That's why they ain't around today; it's the end of the month. Rent day.

I walked over to Niara, snatched her by the hand and dragged her into the bathroom. She needed a bath, but I wasn't going to give her one. Let them do it. They wanted her for the weekend well this was how she came.

I took a wash rag from the wall and turned on the hot and cold water. I did not bother letting the sink basin fill up. I rubbed soap on the rag and then began wiping Niara's face roughly.

"Mummy that hurts," said the little girl.

"Ain't nobody hurting' you-- stand still."

"Soap in my eye."

"Then close your eyes. How do you expect me to clean your face-- just with water?"

"My eye," Niara tried squirming away from my cleansing hands. "I don't want it," she said referring to the washing she was receiving.

"Git back over here," I said.

"No," she said moving away from me. "I don't want it."

"Girl I don't have time for this. If you want to see your grandmother, you better git over here."

"No."

"Who are you talking to?" I said reaching for her. "I told you about telling me no-- didn't I?"

I slapped Niara on the leg. She screamed, jumping up and down in anger. I couldn't hit her as hard as I wanted because she wasn't in my direct reach, but I got my message across.

"Git your black butt over here before I give you a real beating."

"Yes Mummy," she said, but remained standing out of my reach.

I walked over to her and yanked her back in front of the sink, "Don't you move. You hear me?"

"Yes Mummy."

I stuck the rag under the running water and used a bar of soap to create lather. I washed her arms next. I washed her stomach and the front of both legs. Then I did the same to the back parts of her body.

"I want brush teeth."

"I'll do it. You take too long."

"No. I want to do it," she said reaching up for her toothbrush.

"I said no."

I smeared green toothpaste onto a brush and hastily brushed Niara's top ones and then her bottom ones. I tried to brush them at least once a day. I hated to see children with yellow teeth.

"Spit," I said pointing to the sink. "And don't get it on the floor."

I watched my daughter spit. The toothpaste and saliva left her mouth in a drool. Rinsing was even more messy.

"Put your panties on."

Niara attempted to step into them. She stuffed both legs into one opening. She then tried pulling them up, but stopped when she heard me shout, "What are you doing? Not like that-- take one leg out."

"Ahhh!" she cried.

"Cut it out girl. Ain't nobody hit you." I snatched the underwear from her and directed her to put one leg in one opening and then the other leg in the second opening. I helped her pull them up.

"Three-years-old and you can't even put on your panties. Don't make no sense," I mumbled continuing to dress her. I pulled a red short

sleeve shirt over her head and stuffed both of her arms through the sleeves. From the flat surface of the toilet tank, I picked up red socks and blue shorts.

"Here, put these on," I said handing Niara the socks.

I sat on the lid of the toilet and watched impatiently as she sat on the tiled floor and pulled her socks over two small beige feet. She was successful, but the heels of the socks were in the wrong places. I didn't have enough patience left to watch Niara put on her shorts so I interrupted her actions.

"I'll help you put them on. Come here."

"Why?"

"'cause you are taking too long. And your hair's got to be done," I said throwing her into the clothing and stuffing her feet into cheap sneakers.

If they complained about the quality of her footwear, then let them go out and get her something else. I ain't got the money-- seventy dollar sneakers. Especially when all the other bills got to be paid. Why was I thinking like this? Why was I being hard on myself? I shouldn't care what they think? I still didn't know why I let them take my girl every weekend. Oh yes I did. So I could get some time to myself. I looked like crap. I had no man, but I still needed a rest.

"Stop pulling your head away-- I can't make a straight part."

"No-- hurt," she said tugging against me.

"Girl be still," I said popping Niara on the head with the comb.

She cried, but I ignored her and continued parting her hair and braiding it into long black plaits. I made another square part and braided that section too. I did this until all of Niara's hair was plaited. She struggled with me and I popped her whenever I got frustrated.

"Where Grandmah?" she asked watching me put the comb and brush inside the medicine cabinet.

"She'll be here soon."

"I'm going to her house?"

"Don't look so happy-- if you didn't look the way you did, she probably wouldn't give a damn about you. She just wants to show off her pretty granddaughter to all them people in church. Dressing you up like some doll just so they can say how pretty you are."

"Grandmah give me this," she said pointing to the diamond studded earrings in her ears. She was proud. Sticking out her chest, she danced around in the bathroom touching them and smiling.

"You better be glad I don't take them for myself. I could use them better than some kid. I ain't gonna have her spoiling you. I know that much. I'm the one whose got to raise you and I ain't putting up with no nasty, spoiled little girl."

"Grandmah's coming-- we go to Toy Z Us?"

"I don't want no more toys coming in here. We ain't got no more room in this place."

Wrapping Niara's toothbrush in toilet paper, I snatched her towel off the rack and picked up the wet rag on the basin. I shoved them into the plastic grocery bag on the floor. It already contained panties, shorts, shirts, and socks. The wet rag clung to the sides of the bag leaving a moist look.

"Doorbell Mummy," said Niara. *"Grandmah?"*

"Yeah it's her." I didn't have to say come on because Niara was already out of the bathroom and running to the apartment door.

"Don't you open that door!" I screamed after her.

"It's Grandmah. It's Grandmah," she sang, running even faster than before. The apartment wasn't big so she reached it quickly. Her ears didn't absorb my warning because as she reached the door her hands began fumbling with the locks. Niara played with them until she successfully unlocked all of them. Then she opened the door to a crack for the woman on the other side. It was too heavy for her to do more. Grandmah had to open it the rest of the way.

"It's Grandmah!" she said hugging the older woman's legs. *"How are you?"*

41

NIARA

"What's with the questions? Don't Grandmah get a kiss?"

"Yes," said Niara waiting for her big round face to lower so that she could kiss it.

"Mummah," was the noise Niara made as her lips pressed into the thick dark skin of her Grandmother's face.

It was amazing that the older woman's face was still relatively soft considering the thickness of her skin. Maybe it was the fatness that laid underneath. Grandmother's body was not fat, but her face seemed to have more than its normal share of fat cells.

"And mummah to you," Grandmother said mimicking her grandchild's kiss. "Are you happy to see me?"

Niara smiled and nodded her head. That was all she got a chance to do before she heard, "Didn't I tell you not to open that door?"

Niara swung around to look at me; Nancy looked up.

"Calm yourself Cathleen. She knew it was me."

"I don't care. She is not supposed to open the door for anyone."

Niara stood rooted to the spot near her Grandmother in the doorway. She was afraid to move.

"I told you not to open that door," I said pulling her into the living room and away from her imaginary protection. I smacked the backs of her legs with my hand.

"You better start listening to me-- if I tell you not to do something, you better listen. I don't care whose at that door."

"Arrrhhh! Arrhhgg!" screamed Niara running around me in circles. She was trying to escape me, but I wouldn't let go of her hand.

"Why are you beating her like that? I'm her Grandmother. Stop this mess girl," she said walking over to us.

"Don't get in the middle of this," I threatened.

"Arrrhh," Niara continued crying.

"Next time you gonna listen to me girl?" I asked.

Niara did not respond; she just continued to cry.

"Shut up and answer me," I said raising my hand to hit her again.

"Yes Mummy-- yes, I understand," said Niara between hiccups and tears.

"None of this is necessary Cathleen. She knew it was me."

"Look I don't have to explain myself. I don't have to justify anything I do-- Niara go get your bag in the bathroom."

"Why are you so hard on her?"

"'cause it didn't have to be you at the door."

"No? Who do you have coming in here that you need to be afraid to open your own door? I hope you aren't letting those other girls bring all kinds of men in here. Niara doesn't need to be in that kind of environment.

"Their boyfriends are their problems. Niara and I are not around them that much-- but what are you trying to say?" I asked.

"I just don't want nothing to happen to Niara. I'm not trying to imply anything. I know you are doing the best you can. And I know it hasn't been easy."

"I know how to protect my daughter. And I don't need no instructions from anybody-- just because I was stupid enough to get pregnant by your son doesn't mean I'm always gonna be stupid. I don't leave her by herself with no man."

"I'm not accusing you of being stupid--"

"So why are you always doing that? Asking me questions. I ain't afraid of nobody coming to that door. But when I tell Niara something, she'd better listen."

"I'm sorry," said the older woman. I'm just worried about the both of you living here, in this neighborhood. I suppose it comes out in questions like that sometimes. I simply want Niara to have a safe, happy childhood."

"I don't know how happy it's gonna be without a father. Maybe

43

you should go to your son and ask him some questions. Like why he ain't seen his daughter since she's been born? Or how come he don't help support his own kid?"

"I do not have control over my son any more. I wish I did. He doesn't seem to want to hear anything I have to say about Niara."

"It figures. He's a fool," I said dismissing him from my conversation. "Niara! What are you doing in there?"

"I here Mummy," the little girl said walking out of the bathroom. She had toothpaste smeared all over her face.

"I brushed teeth again," she said.

"Go wipe your face and hurry up. Your Grandmother is waiting. Don't forget to go to the pot-pot," I reminded.

I turned the radio on and walked into the kitchen. Nancy followed me. It wasn't a long walk. Our apartment was extremely small. For the eight people living here it was almost unbearable.

"Do you want something to drink?" I asked opening the refrigerator. I took out a pitcher of kool-aide. I then took a glass from the dish rack and poured the liquid into it.

"No."

"Fine," I said.

"Cathleen?" Nancy began hesitantly. She was unsure of her position and did not want to offend her granddaughter's mother again.

"I want to talk to you-- about Niara. I would like to raise her. I know you are doing a good job, but her grandfather and I think we can give her more. A house to grow up in, a good education-- all the things somebody like her deserves," she rushed on wanting to finish her statement before I had a chance to interrupt it.

I simply looked at her. No words came from my mouth. I was not surprised. I had expected her to get around to it sooner or later.

"George and I wouldn't be taking her from you. We would be allowing you time to grow up. You are too young to be doing this all

44

alone. You need to finish high school. I know you do not want to be on Welfare all your life. And that's what will happen if you don't let someone help you."

"I ain't giving you my daughter."

"I am not asking you to. I just want to raise her while you get yourself together. You are only nineteen. You are very young yourself."

"No," I said gulping some of my drink down.

"You can see her any time you want."

"I know I can 'cause she is gonna be right here with me."

"Think Cathleen. What is going to happen if she stays here? She is going to be trapped. You are already trapped. Let me help you. I want Niara to have a future. Let me take her. I can send her to a good public school. We have a great one down the street from us-- it would be just until you got your diploma."

"I said no!"

"If you want to go to college, I could help you."

"Yeah right. And how am I going to do that? I got no money."

"I'll help you with tuition."

I was startled by this comment. "Why should you? I'm nothing to you."

"You're Niara's mother."

"That's nothing," I dismissed her answer.

"At least think about it. You'll have a chance to start over again. You made one mistake. Don't let it ruin your entire life."

"What about your husband? What about Nathaniel?"

"I do not care what Nathaniel thinks. He is off in his own little world. If when he does find out, he doesn't like it; well that's too bad. He has done things I do not approve of either," she said referring to his rejection of Niara. "My husband simply loves his granddaughter. He has already begun turning the guest room into a bedroom for her."

"So you think I'm gonna say yes?"

"I am hoping you will. Like I said just think about it for a while."

I said nothing else. I walked back into the other room to see what Niara was doing. She was playing with her blocks.

"Git your bag," I said pointing to the plastic grocery bag; its opening had been stuffed with bright colored blocks and hard backed books. Obviously additions made by Niara and all of them were gifts given to her by Nancy. I hadn't contributed one educational toy to her small collection; they had all come from Nancy. Would she grow up to be just like me, ignorant? Would she also become pregnant by some nucklehead-- just like me? I didn't want that, but I did not want to give her up either.

"Time to go," I said walking over to her and bending down. "Give Mummy a kiss."

She did as I said, pressing her tiny lips into mine. It was a habit I knew I had to break her out of.

I hugged her hard and asked, "You know Mummy loves you?"

"Yes," said the little girl.

"It's just that I got so much on my mind. All these bills. And I don't have--"

"Money," she completed for me.

I looked at her with surprise in my eyes, "What do you know about money? Have I been complaining about it that much?"

She looked back at me. I could see she liked the reaction her words caused.

"Money Mummy?"

"Yes Mummy needs money," I smiled a little. Maybe things would get better for Niara and myself if I did what Nancy wanted. We couldn't continue to live like this.

I continued talking to my daughter, "I'm sorry about what I said. I shouldn't blame you for something that's not your fault. You are the only family I got."

"Are we going to the park?" she asked oblivious to what I was trying to say.

"I don't know," I said giving up any further effort to explain my actions. She was too young to realize what I had said earlier. I just had to remember not to do it again. Next time she might understand what I was saying and I didn't want to hurt her.

"Give me a hug and I'll ask Grandmother if you can go to the park."

"Okay," she tried to hug me with her short arms. And I did hug her with my longer ones. I tried to hug all the hurtful words away. I felt a choking sensations in my throat. I wanted to cry. How did I get like this? Was my whole life going to continue on this path? And what about Niara? I couldn't let this happen to her.

I knew I was only nineteen, but I wanted to be more of a mother than my own mother had been. I wanted to be in my daughter's life. I wanted to teach her-- take her to the zoo, and the library. I wanted us to go on trips. I wanted her to have the love my mother didn't bother showing me.

"See you Monday," I said standing up.

"Park Grandmah?" Niara asked walking to the older woman.

"If that is what you want."

"Yes," said the little girl.

"Goodbye Mummy," she said looking back at me as she and her grandmother were getting ready to leave.

"Bye," I said.

"Take your time thinking about it. There is no rush," said Nancy. "I know it's going to be a hard decision to make."

"I don't know. Maybe I will think about it."

"Goodbye Cathleen," said Nancy closing the front door behind her...

CHAPTER TWO

'Please put some more ice in my glass Niara,"...
'Could you cut me a slice of that chocolate cake dear?'
'I need a coupla Tylenols Niara. This headache is getting worse,'...
'Any more coffee left?'

If one more Great Aunt or Great Uncle or first cousin, or neighbor or friend of the family told me to get them one more glass of ice or piece of cake or cup of coffee or glass of water or Tylenol because their stomach couldn't tolerate aspirin, I was going to snap. Right here, in the middle of this living room. I was not going to give a warning; I was just going to tell them to 'get up and get it yourself!'

All day long, since people have been coming back to the house from the funeral, I have been acting like a servant. I've been getting them this and getting them that.

A lot of them acted like a party was going on instead of a funeral. I could hear laughter in many corners of the house. I knew many of them were grieving over Grandmother's death, but it still made me uncomfortable to hear the cheerfulness in the air.

I expected the house to be quiet with mourning. I expected more crying, but that was not what was going on. People were remembering stories of when Grandmother was a little girl or when she first met Grandfather or some other funny event in her life.

When were they going to leave? It was already after eleven o'clock. I understood that many of them traveled far to get

48

here, but I still could not wait until they left. I wanted to leave all the noise behind. I wanted to go into my bedroom and cry. My grandmother was dead. The woman who loved me, who took me to the park when I was small, who insisted that I become a girl scout, who signed me up for modern dance class, who cleaned up my vomit whenever I did not make it to the bathroom, who explained my period to me, who bought me my first bra, who told me not to have sex until I got married, who made me go to church whether I felt like it or not... was dead. She was gone. And her love for me was gone. It no longer existed. I could feel the tears forming in my eyes and my nose began to run. I sniffed real hard trying to keep the mucus from running out.

My grandmother was gone; she would never see me go on my senior prom or graduate from high school. She would never get a chance to inspect my first boyfriend-- and I would never be able to tell her about my first kiss. I cried at these thoughts. I looked around the room for a tissue box.

Why did she have to die? Why did she have to get breast cancer? Why didn't anybody feel the lump? Why didn't the doctors find it earlier? I thought when they removed both breasts everything was going to be all right, but then the doctors said it had spread too far for them to do anything else. I hated seeing her in all that pain. I knew she had to die, but I still had a hard time accepting it.

I quietly left the living room and headed for the kitchen. I pushed the glass door blocking its entrance and walked through the threshold. I felt very drained. From the moment I got up and got dressed (skipping breakfast), to the funeral and burial, I had not stopped once to rest. I even helped the women from my church cook the dinner. We prepared fried chicken, baked chicken, ham, pork chops, collard greens, mustard greens, rice and gravy, potato salad, candied yams...

It had been a long day-- and seeing my mother had not helped one bit. Why had she come? I was surprised to see her and even more surprised that she had the nerve to sit with Grandfather and me.

As I thought about Cathleen, I picked up a dirty fork and began scraping the food from the plates that seemed to be everywhere. It was probably going to take all night to clean the kitchen or even to see the whiteness of the countertop again. Greasy smudges were on everything: glasses, plates, forks, spoons, cabinets, walls. Maybe by the time I finished in here all of my family would be gone. I hoped so.

I opened the dishwasher door and pulled out the top rack. Stacking the dirty cups and glasses in the rack was going to be the easy part, because I only had to rinse them. But the silverware was something else, food particles were sticking to them making it difficult to clean. I filled the sink with hot water and put the forks, knives, and spoons in to soak. I then grabbed the stack of dishes I had just scraped and put them in the sink. Most of this stuff needed to soak.

I was glad I didn't have on long sleeves, because if I did I would be constantly pushing them up in order to keep them out of the dish water.

"I didn't know you were in here," my Grandfather spoke from the doorway. He was carrying a cup balanced on a saucer. He walked over to the stove and lightly touched the kettle.

"It's not hot," I said walking over to the kitchen table. I removed the remainder of dirty dishes and wiped the crumbs onto the floor. I'd sweep and mop it before I went to bed.

"Did everybody leave?" I asked.

"Just about. My sister and brother have decided to stay a few weeks-- 'til everything is settled. The will has to be read."

"Oh," I walked back to the sink. I dipped the dishcloth into the lukewarm water and began wiping the food spills from the countertop. The kitchen was looking a little better. I don't know how long it took to get to this point, but I was glad I was making progress.

He spoke again, "I didn't expect Cathleen to blurt out our decision like that."

The kettle whistled letting us know the water was hot. He poured himself a cup and then added two tablespoons of instant coffee. He lightened it with creamer and took a sip. Grandfather did not bother to move away from the stove.

"I wanted to talk to you first-- to explain things."

I stopped working to look at him.

"Explain what?"

"I'm getting old Niara. I won't be around forever--"

"Don't say that. I don't want to hear it," I wanted to stick my soapy fingers in my ears. I really didn't want to hear anything else about dying.

"I know Niara, but one day I am going to die too," he said.

"And I do not want to leave you here all alone-- with no family."

"That won't happen. I got family."

"Most of them are old just like me. I want to make sure you will be taken care of when I'm gone. Hadn't really thought about it until Nancy died."

51

I wanted to say Grandfather you aren't going anywhere. You are going to be around for a long time. But I couldn't say it because, I didn't know if it was true. So I kept my mouth shut and listened.

"I always thought your father would step in and eventually take over raising you. I cannot understand why he's refused to do that. I know he and your mother don't get along, but that's no reason to ignore you-- whatever their differences are."

"It doesn't matter anymore. I don't care about either of them," I said.

"I hope you don't mean that," he said.

"Why shouldn't I? They don't care about me. Cathleen's never been around for me. And the last time I stayed with Father all we did was argue. He didn't really want me there. And his wife doesn't like me either. She didn't want me to touch anything in her precious house. How was I supposed to stay there for a month and not use her washing machine or dryer?"

"It's ridiculous for an adult to act like that," Grandfather declared.

"Did she expect me to walk to the laundry mat? Well I wasn't going to do that. I don't care what nobody said. But you know what really gets me? Not once did Father stand up for me. I was always the one in the wrong. It was never Shelby. I was his daughter long before she was his wife. Don't that count for something?"

"It should, but we can't change him. He's got to do that by himself."

"I doubt that will happen-- anyway who cares. I'll be grown soon."

"Well don't write him off completely Niara."

"It's too late. I've already waited too long."

"We'll see," said Grandfather. "But right now I think we should talk about your mother. I want you to spend the summer with her."

"What-- what did you say?"

"I think you should get to knew her."

"Is that what she meant when we were back at the church? She can forget it. I don't want to know her."

"I'm sorry Niara, but it has been decided. I am going to South Carolina in a few weeks to visit some family. I need to get out of this house. It's too depressing here without Nancy."

"Can I go with you?"

"It's better that you spend the time with your mother."

"What did she say about all this?" I demanded.

"She wants you to come."

"Oh after all this time she suddenly wants me to come and stay with her-- just like that? I won't do it. I don't want to see her again."

"Give her a chance Niara. Things weren't easy for her. She thought she was doing the right thing by letting us raise you."

"So where has she been all this time? How come she never been here to see me? Or even called?"

"I do not have an answer for you."

"And I don't have no rap for a mother who did that to me either."

"You are being too hard on her."

"No I'm not. How else should I feel?"

"I don't know, but you still need a mother. I have talked

things over with Cathleen and she will be here Friday night. She is coming to pick you up."

"Huh? What?" I was totally stunned. "This Friday? All this was decided without anybody talking to me?"

"I am talking to you."

"What good is that now? Everything is set."

"Yes it is, but you still can express how you feel. I know this is going to be hard on you."

"So why are you doing it? She's got no business coming back into my life-- none!"

"But she's your mother--"

"It means nothing to me."

"You may not agree Niara, but reestablishing a relationship with her is important for you."

"No it's not."

"One day you might need her," said Grandfather.

"I hope not. Because if I do, she'll probably let me down again."

"You will only be with her for the summer," he said trying to appeal to me. "That's not a long time. Try to get to know her. She might not be all that bad."

"Can I go now?" I asked wanting to put an end to this conversation. "I'll finish cleaning the kitchen in the morning."

"Go ahead Niara. I'll sweep up here and put out the trash."

"Night," I said walking out of the room with my head down. He couldn't really be telling me to forgive my mother for not loving me. If she had, she would not have given me away. No I didn't want to reestablish anything with her. She wasn't my mother and she could never be my mother.

54

I was too tired to wash my face and hands or do any of my normal preparations for bed. I just walked into my room and threw myself across the bed; I didn't undress. Or bother turning out the light. I just fell asleep with my arms and legs dangling over the sides of the bed. And, my face was crushed against my pillows.

If she wanted me to live with her, she was going to have to drag me from this room kicking and screaming. I wasn't going out any other way.

CHAPTER THREE

I wish I had kept my promise. I wish I had put up a fight--made Cathleen drag me out of my room, but I didn't. I couldn't upset Grandfather like that so I left my room like a whipped puppy. I walked out passively, but I refused to acknowledge her. There was no way I could say anything to her without me getting really ugly. So I kept my mouth shut.

I carried all my boxes and suitcases out to the car and kissed Grandfather goodbye. I made him swear to call me when he got to South Carolina. I even begged him to change his mind, but he wouldn't.

He said, "No Niara. I think this is best for you," and then kissed me on my cheek.

I refused to look at the woman who had come for me. She didn't deserve even that level of respect. So I ignored her. I got into the passenger's seat and slammed the car door. I was hoping I'd slammed it so hard that the door would fall off its hinges. Then maybe she'd change her mind. Of course, that didn't happen. So I settled for putting on my earphones and drowning out any awareness of her by turning up the music as high as it would go.

She didn't say a word to me. Instead she started the car; we drove away. No attempt at speaking was made until she angrily reached across the seat and snatched the earphones out of my walkman.

"Trying to ignore me is not going to change the situation,"

said Cathleen, taking her eyes off the street to look at me.

"I got nothing to say to you."

"Don't you want to know where we are going?"

"No."

"Did your Grandfather tell you anything about me?"

"Yes."

"Did he say why you are coming to stay with me?"

"Yes," I said. I was anxious to end any communication with this woman.

"George feels that you and I--"

"I'm tired of talking. When are you going to be finished?"

"Look Niara, I know this isn't easy for you, but let's not start off wrong."

"Don't tell me how to behave. We started off wrong years ago."

"I had my reasons for doing that," she explained.

"Please, before you even start. I don't want to hear them. All that matters is that you did it and that's that."

"But I want you to understand why."

"No. You understand this. I don't like you and I'm not going to."

"That's a real nice thing to say. Is that supposed to make me angry? Are you trying to make me change my mind about having you live with me?"

"Have you?"

"No."

"Fine," I dismissed her.

"Aren't you curious about where you'll be living?"

"No."

"Well I'm going to tell you anyway. I have a house in Philadelphia--"

"Probably in some ghetto," I muttered.

"I guess you really do hate me?"

"You don't have to guess."

"You've got a very nasty mouth Niara. You weren't that way as a little girl."

"How do you know? You wasn't around that long."

"I was with you until you were three."

'Oh now I'm supposed to be impressed? You were there for me for three whole big years-- how can I thank you Cathleen? Tell me what I should do."

"Don't talk to me like that."

"I'll say what I want. I'm not a child anymore in case you hadn't noticed," I plugged my earphones back into the walkman. If she wanted to talk she could talk to herself. I was finished with this conversation.

We continued the rest of the ride in semi-silence. I listened to the walkman and said nothing. She drove over some bridge I didn't know the name of and into Philadelphia.

The city looked dirty. Trash was dumped on the sides of the roads. Littered paper and beer bottles were everywhere. The trail of debris seemed to follow us all the way to the little row house we eventually pulled up in front of. I definitely was not impressed. It was a tacky looking house hidden by white aluminum siding. The steps were severely cracked. If I wasn't careful, I could see myself falling into them and disappearing forever.

For the first time I looked directly at her and spoke, "You

have got to be kidding? I'm not supposed to live there, am I?"

"I haven't been living here long-- I bought the place six months ago. I am fixing it up a little at a time-- the steps will be the next thing I'll get repaired."

"I'm going to have to live here for three months? In this run down dump-- does it look that bad inside?"

"You have a nice room," she said evading my question.

"I guess it does."

"Get your things from the trunk."

"Do I have to?"

"Yes," she said as I was walking to the back of her car.

I should have known by the gray car she was driving that her house looked bad. Her car looked like it had been new in 1973. It had rust all around the trunk and sides . I hadn't really looked at it before. I'd been too angry. But looking at it now, I was embarrassed to even stand next to it. She must really be poor if she drives something like this.

It was one car I definitely didn't want to be seen in again. And as if to emphasize my feelings, I quickly lifted the trunk and reached inside for my bags. I brought with me four leather bags full of clothes and a lot of cardboard boxes; the boxes were full of clothes and shoes and body products...

By the time I had unloaded the trunk, Cathleen had gotten out and was leading the way up the cracked steps. I followed her. She unlocked the door and I walked into the house. I couldn't see anything until she flipped on the light. And then, I saw a small living room. It was neat but everything looked old. The carpet, the couch, the wallpaper, the coffee table. It looked like she had furnished the whole room with stuff she'd bought in a Salvation

Army Store. I couldn't believe my eyes. Was I supposed to live here? In this cheap looking house?

"You can take your things upstairs while I park the car. Your room is at the end of the hall."

"I hope it doesn't look as tired as this," I said carrying my heavy bags upstairs.

I made three trips up and down the stairs before I had everything piled up against one wall in the room; I wasn't about to unpack anything. I was too tired-- and I didn't belong here. I stretched out across the bed and hoped I wouldn't catch anything. I also hoped Cathleen would leave me alone now that all my stuff was moved in. I didn't want to talk to her-- not tonight. But I guess my hoping was in vain, because she walked into the room as I was staring down at the floor. The carpet in here was a tacky blue. It was just about as flat as my chest was.

"I'm glad you are here," she said awkwardly.

"I don't know what for. I'm not here because I want to be. Grandpah made me come."

"I'm still glad you're here."

"Yeah, okay."

"Do you have any questions?"

"Not really," I said disinterested.

"I guess you are wondering where I've been all these years?"

"Not anymore," I said. "I stopped trying to figure that out a long time ago-- it's not important now."

"Maybe not to you, but I want you to know anyway."

"Go ahead. Tell me if you want. It's not going to make a difference now."

60

"I guess you know I was sixteen when I got pregnant?"

"Yeah I know that. Grandmah told me."

"Did she tell you that I had to raise you by myself-- since your father wasn't around?"

"I know that too."

"Trying to take care of a small baby is real hard on somebody sixteen-- I did it for a while, but then your grandmother offered to take you for a while. Until I got myself together--"

"I can see that never happened," I mumbled.

She ignored me and continued speaking, "At first I rejected the offer, but later on I realized it was the right thing to do. I didn't want you to live the same life I did. I wanted you to finish school-- not be limited 'cause of the place you grew up in."

"So what happened? Where have you been?" I asked.

"In and out of different clinics," she said truthfully. "I started messing with drugs soon after you left. I thought it was no big deal-- I did just a little here and there."

"You became an addict?" I said incredulously.

"No at first. It didn't seem to affect me, but soon I was using it a lot. Didn't mean to get hooked."

"I guess it was crack?" I asked.

"No. Crack is today's problem. Back then it was heroin. I was depressed. A few girlfriends were doing it. Said it would make me forget all about everything, so I tried it."

"Boy!" I looked at Cathleen. "You really are dumb. Doing heroin? Didn't you know how bad that stuff was?"

"No I didn't."

"You really are stupid!"

"I know that now."

"You should have known it back then."

"Well I didn't," she said defensively.

"So what happened to you?"

"I got strung out and that's when your Grandmother stopped hearing from me."

"You've been an addict for twelve years?"

"No. I've been clean for four."

"Does Grandpah know what you are?"

"Were," she corrected. "He knows I am recovering."

"And he still wants me to get to know you?" I asked in obvious disdain.

"I asked him not to tell you. I wanted to be the person you heard it from."

"And he listened to you?"

"He did, because I've changed. No more drugs. I'm not making excuses Niara. I just want you to know the truth. My life hasn't been easy."

"Neither has mine," I said.

"I'm sorry."

"Don't be. I had other people around to help me."

"I'm not proud of the past, but I want to start over again with you."

"You are wasting your time. I don't want to start over. I don't want nothing."

"I want you to understand things."

"Does it matter now?"

"To me," she said.

"That's your problem then, not mine."

"I know you are mad at me, but give me a chance. I know I

made a lot of mistakes but, I can't change that. All I can do is go on from here."

"I'm not asking you to change. It was your life. You did what you wanted."

"I was only sixteen back then. I didn't know anything. I was young and dumb."

"So I keep hearing," I said rolling onto my back. I was tired of looking at her and I was tired of hearing excuses. Let her tell them to somebody else. I wasn't interested in hearing them anymore. I'm almost grown and the last thing I needed was a mother coming back into my life. I don't need her now. I wanted to feel sorry for her, but I couldn't. I couldn't get pass all the years I waited for her to come and get me. I couldn't get pass all the times I cried because of her. I refused to forgive her for any of the pain she'd caused me.

Cathleen spoke, breaking into my thoughts, "Do you spend a lot of time with your father?"

"Same amount I spent with you," I said sarcastically. "He's living in New York and he doesn't have time for me either."

"Oh."

"Are you finished yet?"

"I guess I am," she said and walked out of the room.

I should have been extremely happy that she was leaving me alone, but I wasn't. I felt a sadness inside that I was reluctant to admit. I didn't want to understand anything she had to say. I wanted to continue to hate her as I did for all those years she never bothered to think about me. I wanted to be invincible where she was concerned. I could not allow her or anybody else to hurt me again.

NIARA

So I laid on the bed watching her leave. I was being tough. I would not show her any emotion. I was not going to be weak or break down because she told me some sad story. Those were the decisions she chose to make, now she was going to have to live with them.

I closed my eyes. I just wanted to rest for a moment; I was tired. I intended to get up and put on my night clothes, but instead I fell asleep.

CHAPTER FOUR

The next day came quickly. I didn't sleep that well. And I was hungry. I was sitting on the floor in the room that was designated mine when I heard her footsteps stop on the cheap carpeting at its entrance.

I heard her voice, but I did not look up. I was writing my first letter to Grandfather. I planned to write him once a week. My chin was slightly touching my chest because I was bent forward.

" I left stew on the stove for you," she said. "--if you get hungry."

"I already ate," I lied.

"When did you eat?" she challenged me. "You haven't left this room once today."

"Don't need to," I said casually. "I brought my own food-- enough to last for months," again I was lying. I wish I had thought far enough ahead to know I would need food, but I had been too preoccupied with hating her to do that.

"If you change your mind, it's there."

"I won't."

"I'm leaving," she said. "I'm going to a meeting. I left the phone number on the table in case you need to reach me."

"To a meeting?"

"It's a support group. I'm going to tell them about you."

"You need that?" I asked. "I thought you were off the stuff."

"I am, but I still want to stay in touch with them. And they are excited about you coming to live with me."

"Oh," was all I could say.

"I'll be stopping at the supermarket. Do you want me to get you something?"

"No."

"Nothing? No chips? No ice cream?"

"Don't talk to me like I'm some kid."

Now it was her turn to be at a lost for words, "I-- I wasn't trying to do that. I'm sorry."

"Offering me ice cream isn't going to make me like you," I warned. "And for your information I like frozen yogurt. Don't look surprised. There's a lot you don't know about me," I said going back to my letter writing.

"I'll be back in a few hours," she said waiting for a response.

"You can go now. I heard what you had to say," I remarked condescendingly. "You're going to a meeting, then shopping and you'll be back in a couple of hours-- right?"

"And my phone number is--"

"On the kitchen table," I interrupted.

"I'm leaving," she said shaking her head and exiting my room with a stiff back.

Good. She was gone, but what was I going to do for three months? I looked around the room. If I stayed in here, I'd go crazy. That was definitely out. I'd have to find something to do-- boy was I hungry. I was still living on yesterday's food.

I needed food and I needed it bad. There had to be a supermarket around here somewhere. I got up from the floor, located my handbag and walked to the mirror. I hadn't washed today, but I didn't smell-- at least not yet. I checked my eyes for sleep and licked my pointing finger with my tongue. I erased any evidence of sleep from my mouth with it. I undid my ponytail and searched my handbag until I found a comb. I combed it and put it back into its previous style.

I am not an ignorant or dirty person, but I was not going to use any of this woman's stuff. I would rather stink; I would prefer to look dirty than accept anything from her.

Once I had finished checking the mirror, I walked down the stairs and out of the door. I had no qualms about leaving her front door unlocked. There was nothing in it worth stealing-- at least not down here.

I wasn't sure where I was going, but I felt like I was regaining a little control back over my life. I found a corner mini-market not too far from the house. I bought a hoagie and a soda. Then I reluctantly returned to the house.

Not speaking to Cathleen became the norm for me, I preferred it that way. I did not feel like pretending with her. But when it was necessary to talk to her, it was always brief; it was often lopsided. I was always the angry one and she was always the one trying to establish a relationship.

Cathleen tried to tolerate my refusal to eat her food, but I knew how to get to her. I would tell her as bluntly as I could that I wasn't going to eat anything in her house. I would rather starve. Then I would dramatically marched down to the corner store and buy my breakfast, lunch, or dinner. This depended on what time the argument occurred. She accepted this behavior for a while, but her patience soon began to wear thin as the weeks moved on. And as her patience thinned, our battles began to grow more intense. I

should have also realized it would only be a matter of time before
she insisted that I unpack the cardboard boxes lining my wall. She
was not going to accept their presence forever.
I was sitting on the bed, in the tiny room, staring at them
one day when Cathleen walked in.
"I know you've got a problem with being here, but leaving
your stuff in them boxes ain't going to change anything."
"It might," I said looking at her.
"When are you going to unpack them?"
"I'm not--"
"So you're just going to sit there staring at them for another
day?"
"If I feel like it."
"I'm tired of this. How long are you going to act like this,
girl?"
"Long enough to get on your nerve I hope."
"I'm not going to keep playing games with you, Niara.
This childish stuff is not going to make the summer go faster. Why
don't you go outside. Walk around, see where everything is. You
can bypass Turner's mini-market though considering you go there
every day," she said attempting to be funny, but it was lost on me.
"What for? So I can get robbed? I'm not going outside
unless I have to."
I didn't really feel that way, but I said it to irk her, however
my words didn't seem to affect her. If they did, she hid it well.
"The girls across the street have been asking about you.
They want you to come over."
"So what. I don't know them."
"I told them I had a daughter. And they want to meet you.

68

Why don't you go over there today?"

"Don't call me that," I lashed out. "I'm not your daughter."

Why are you so angry? I told you I did what I had to do. It wasn't easy for me to make that decision."

"Just like it wasn't easy for you to make the decision to do drugs? Auh forget it. What's the point in talking about it now. Just don't call me your daughter, okay?"

"But that's who you are."

"No!" I yelled. "Not no more. If anybody asks me, I'll tell them I don't have a mother. Don't expect me to act like your daughter-- because I'm not."

"Say what you want. I don't really care. I'm getting tired of you. You can act like a baby if you want, but you are still my daughter. And you are still going to live with me. Get use to the idea," said Cathleen walking from the room.

"I'm tired of you too! I wish you'd just walk right out of my life!"

"Keep on wishing, because it ain't happening here."

"I got to get out of here," I said getting up from the floor. "Damn I stink," I said lifting my arms and taking a sniff.

I didn't really need to lift them to smell the odor. If I was going to do anything today, I definitely had to take a bath. I guess I would have to do it here-- whether I wanted to or not. Up until this point, I refused to use anything in the house that belonged to her-- unless it was absolutely necessary. That meant no food, no television, no outgoing phone calls, no baths...

But if she really wanted me to live here, then that's what I'm going to do. I still refused to unpack the boxes; I rummaged through them until I found a pair of jeans and a white shirt and argyle socks and a hairbrush. Where were my loafers? In the box with my books. I reclosed the boxes and headed for the bathroom.

Once inside that tiny bathroom, I grabbed a towel and washcloth from the closet. I ran water in the tub and then got undressed. Wherever the clothes hit the floor was where they were going to remain. If she wanted me then she got me, bad habits and all. Even though, I was not really a sloppy person-- at least not until now.

I took a quick bath, let the water out of the tub and got dressed. It was the quickest bath I had ever taken, but if I had to do it here then I wanted it to be quick. I couldn't stand using her water, or anything that she owned. I brushed my hair into a ponytail, deliberately leaving strands of black hair in the sink. Let her clean that up too, I thought smiling into the mirror.

As I left the bathroom, I made sure it looked a mess. I left a greasy ring in the tub, water puddles on the tiled floor, and my dirty clothes all over the floor. I walked down the stairs and out the front door.

I was hungry so I headed for Turner's mini-market. After that, maybe I'd go for a walk. It would be better than staying in that house with her for another day. All she did was bug me, "Why are you spending all your money buying hoagies? I got lots of food in the refrigerator." Or, "Come downstairs, I rented a movie for you." Of course, I had responses for her requests. I would say, " I don't want your food." Or, "How do you know what movies I like?" Then I'd slam the door before she tried to say something else. I knew she hated that, but too bad. I hated being here and I couldn't do a thing about it. So, I did not care how she felt.

I walked into Turner's mini-market. The building occupied

one corner of a long, narrow city block. I went inside and headed for the refrigerator. I picked up a beverage.

"How much is this?" I asked holding up a bottle of apple juice. Normally I would buy the two liter soda, but my money was short now.

"A dollar twenty."

"Oh," I said putting it back behind the glass enclosure.
"And this?" I asked holding up a bottle of soda.

The man looked up again from whatever he was doing behind the register and said, "Seventy-five cents."

I put that back too.

"Can sodas are fifty-cents," he added.

"Oh," I repeated, moving to the refrigerator that contained them. I reached around the pineapple. I never tried that before. My hands settled on grape. I walked to the counter and waited quietly for the man to look up. He did after a moment of writing something down.

"Do you want anything clsc?" hc askcd politcly.

"A hoagie."

"What kind do you want?"

"Italian," I usually got roast-beef with cheese, but now I had to watch what I bought. Maybe I should ask the man if the store was hiring.

IIe made movements in the direction of the deli, but my next words halted him.

"How much are the smalls?" I asked; my tone was a soft one. I usually got large, but my money was running out.

"Smalls are two sixty-five. And larges are three twenty."
I figured out the price of the small and a soda. I could

afford that and I would still have about twenty dollars left.

"Can I have a small?"

"Sure thing," he said entering   the deli area. He washed his hands carefully before he took out the meats necessary for making the hoagie.

"Everything on it?"

"No peppers. No onions. Extra mayonnaise."

"Oil?"

"A little," I said.

"Oregano?"

"Yes."

"You just move around here?" he asked.

"No-- I am only going to be here for the summer."

"Staying with family?"

"Yeah, I guess you can say that."

"Aren't you sure?" he asked eyeing me. "Either you are or you aren't"

"I'm supposed to be staying with my mother."

"You don't sound too thrilled with that situation," he commented viewing my with an even closer stare.

"I'm not. Nobody asked me what I wanted. They all decided what was best for me and now I have to deal with it until the summer is over."

"Maybe things will work themselves out," he said wrapping the hoagie in white paper and eventually taping it.

"I doubt it."

"What's your name?"

"Nia--" I stopped short of answering him. Why did he ask that? Was I talking too much? I didn't want to be telling all my business.

"Why?"

"I like to know the names of the people who come into my store. Mine's Samuel."

"You own this?" I was a little surprised.

"Yes I do," he said proudly. "It's been mine for six years now. Don't be so surprised."

"I didn't know-- I just thought you worked here."

"Don't tell me you're another person who thinks a black man can't own his own business," he teased.

"I didn't say that."

"No but you thought it," he continued gently.

"Sorry."

"No need to be. Now you know differently," he said wiping down the section of the counter he was using before following me to the cash register.

"You still haven't told me your name."

"It's Niara."

"Is that Swahili?" he asked.

"What?"

"Your name."

"I don't know. My mother named me." I didn't mean to say that. What I meant to say was Cathleen.

He continued, "It's been a while since I studied it, but I believe it means destiny or purpose."

"It does?" I asked excitedly.

"Yes."

I paused for a moment and then asked, "Why would you want to learn Swahili?" His answer did not come immediately. He considered it first. Then he spoke. "I wanted to speak it," he corrected. "I wanted a language that was my own. A language whose sounds and intricacies touched my soul and seared my heart with patriotic emotions. I needed my own words, axioms, phrases-- my own tongue. I would often hear Africans from places like Ghana, Botswana, and Senegal speaking in their native language. And I would feel a pride welling up inside of me. I would listen to them and realize I had something before America. I had an identity. I had a people. I had a language. That's why I learned to speak Swahili."

I was silent. I didn't know what to say. How did I feel about being an American? I knew about slavery and I knew it was wrong, but beyond that I hadn't really thought about it. Or the consequences of it. I hadn't thought about losing a language. Or being deprived of an identity. Or what we lost when we were taken from Africa.

"Damn Sam!" exclaimed a man behind me. "You got that written down somewhere. Sounds like you're giving a speech. All I came in here for was a juice and the newspaper. And now you got me feeling all disenfranchised-- like a black man without a land."

"Didn't mean to give a speech. Simply expressing how I feel. That's all."

"You go right ahead brother. Teach'em while they are young."

"I'm doing my best," he said allowing a transparent smile to spread across his face. It revealed the sincerity of his words.

Samuel rung my stuff up, "Three fifteen."

As I handed him the money, a girl about my age rushed into

the store. She was huffing and puffing and definitely out of breath. I was distracted from her as Samuel gave me my change. I picked up my bag and moved away from the register. I was in no rush to go, so I picked up a hair magazine and began flipping through the pages. I could hear the other two speaking in the background.

"I'm sorry I'm late," I heard the girl say. "I know it's the second time this week, but I couldn't help it. I couldn't leave my brother at home all by himself."

"Where was your mother?"

"Atlantic City."

"The casinos?"

"Yup. She just got back this morning. I told her I had to work today, but I guess she just forgot."

"No she didn't. She doesn't care if you get to work late or not."

"She cares. It's just that she said she was winning and she forgot all about the time."

"How much this time?"

"Five hundred dollars," the girl bragged. "She gave me fifty."

The girl patted her hip pocket for show and walked into the register area. She tucked her leather bag somewhere underneath the counter.

"She's not going to be happy until I fire you."

"You wouldn't do that. I work too hard for you."

"That's what you believe, but you better be glad you showed up when you did. I was about to dig out the 'help wanted' sign."

"Don't even try it," she said pulling on a blue apron with

the name Turner's mini-market stitched heavily into the material.

"Tell your mother I need reliable workers. I can't have them coming to work two or three hours late. You got me?"

"Yes Mr. Turner. I'll tell her that."

"And tell her to stop spending all of her money in those casinos. I know she can find something better to do with it."

I stopped listening. I didn't see a hair style I liked so I placed the magazine back in the rack. I was starving. I could smell the meats and cheeses through the bag and I could not resist the urge to see what this new neighborhood had to offer.

I left the mini-market quickly and headed back down Chester Avenue.

CHAPTER FIVE

This morning Cathleen and I argued again. She accused me of ignoring her. She said I should show her a little respect, but I can't see why. She didn't deserve any. She ought to be glad that I even put up with her. A stranger walking down the street was entitled to more respect than she was.

So the minute she started to get loud with me, I walked out of the house. I refused to listen to her screaming about how hard her life had been. I didn't want to hear her excuses. I didn't believe them either.

So this is how I ended up sitting in a dirty park early one morning. I wished I had my Grandmother to talk to. I missed her so much. Right now I had no one.

"I can tell you're not from around here," said a black girl about my age.

I looked up at her; she was a few steps away from me. I was sitting on a bench sipping a mountain dew and munching on chips.

"What's it to you?"

"Nothing really. I was wondering why you were sitting in here."

"You were watching me?" I asked cautiously.

"I thought something was wrong. Not too many people come in this park-- only the addicts."

"I was about to leave," I said.

"Where are you from?"

"That's my business."

"Fine with me, but you shouldn't have your bag lying there wide open like that. Anybody who wants to can get your wallet with no problem."

"There's nothing in it," I said gathering it closer to me and snapping the flap down.

"Don't matter. Empty ones get snatched just as fast as the ones with money in them. A thief can't tell the difference."

"I wasn't really thinking when I said that. Thanks," I said feeling a little stupid.

"It's nothing. I just don't like to see people get taken," she paused. "Are you from Mount Erie? You look like one of them girls? Is that where you're from?"

"No. New Jersey-- Canton Circle."

"Don't know where that's at, but it sounds like money to me."

"My grandparents don't have-- I mean didn't have money. At least not as much as most of the people living there."

"Do you got friends here?"

"No. I'm here because my Grandmah died. I'm living with Cathleen."

"Who's that?" she had no problem asking.

"She's supposed to be my mother."

"Supposed to be? Sounds like you don't like her too much."

"I don't."

"If she's anything like mine, I can understand why."

"I doubt that there is anyone like her-- she's ridiculous. I

78

don't want to talk about her anymore-- what's your name?"

"Kelli."

"I'm Niara."

"That's a nice chain. Is it real?" she asked checking out my gold chain and locket. It was a gift from my Grandmother; I wore it so much I sometimes forgot I had it on.

"No," I said cautiously.

"It sure looks like it."

"I know. Lots of people keep telling me that."

"Where'd your get it?" she asked eyeing it.

"It was a present. Why so many questions-- you act like you want to snatch it,' I said looking her in the eye.

"Ah no," she said laughing slightly off rhythm. "I just haven't' seen one like that."

"Check out the department stores sometime. They probably got plenty of them," I said lifting up the metal chain and dropping it inside my shirt. It was barely visible now.

"Thought it wasn't real?"

"It's not."

Kelli sat down next to me. She was smiling at me. "If I was like that, I'd have the chain on by now."

That's what you think!

"Can I have some?" asked Kelli sticking out her hand.

"I ate most of them," I said handing her the bag.

"Thanks," she said lifting the bag to her mouth and tilting it so that the last bit of chips slid down the sides of the bag and onto her tongue.

"They got to be contacts," the girl said unexpectedly.

"What?"

"Your eyes. I've never seen anybody with them that color before."

Was she laughing at me? Did she think I was trying to be white?

"You're wrong."

"Don't even try it," said Kelli leaning closer to me in order to inspect my face further. "I wish I had green eyes like that."

"Why?"

"So I can be pretty."

"My eyes don't make me pretty," I said seriously. "Your eyes are just as nice."

"I was thinking about getting colored contacts."

"What for?"

"They'd make me stand out-- I don't want to look like everybody else."

"But you don't."

"Sometimes I feel like I do."

"Don't waste your money. There's nothing wrong with your eyes."

"But boys like green eyes-- when the guys around here see you, they're all going to go crazy."

"I don't know what for. I'm not looking for a boyfriend."

"Do you already got one?"

"No."

"Then that ain't gonna mean nothing to them. They are still going to be on you. And I'm telling you, they all got girlfriends. Big, bad girlfriends. They ain't gonna like you stealing their boyfriends either."

"But I'm not."

"Try telling them that-- I bet they're gonna want to kick your butt."

"Why? I don't want anybody's boyfriend."

"It don't matter. All they got to do is see you and that's it. They are going to be jealous-- instantly. Might even try cutting your hair or something."

"I don't believe you," I said becoming frightened. I was tired of jealous girls. I had to deal with them at my school last year. They did not try to cut my hair, but they refused to be my friend. They never invited me to hang out with them after school. I'm sure part of it was because, I'm black. But, I think my looks also had something to do with it. The boys were different. They always treated me friendly. A few even asked me out, but I said no. I wasn't looking for a boyfriend.

"Don't believe me. You'll find out quick enough."

"I got to go," I said standing up. I had enough of this conversation. And I had enough of this strange girl. I was ready to leave her and this dirty park behind. I looked for a trash can to throw my soda container in. I didn't want to hold it until I got home. I spotted one and tossed it inside.

She started laughing, "Wait a minute. I was only kidding 'bout the girls cutting your hair. You deserved it-- acting so stuck up. I wasn't going to snatch your chain."

"That wasn't funny."

"No, but the look on your face was. I didn't know black girls could turn pale," she laughed a little more.

"I guess I did deserve that."

"You did, but forget it," she said. "What are you doing later on?"

"Nothing," I said.

"Why don't you let me show you around the neighborhood. I'm working today, but I get off at six."

"I don't know about that."

"Come on Niara. I know you can use some friends. I can show you who's okay and who is not."

"You're right, I do need a friend," I said smiling. "Okay."

"Good," Kelli smiled.

"Where do you work?"

"At Turner's mini-market."

"You do?" I wondered if she had ever waited on me. Then I remembered the girl who rushed into the store late one afternoon, because her mother was winning at the casinos.

"That's where I've seen you at-- the mini-market. I thought you looked familiar."

"I don't remember seeing you at Turner's," she said.

"Probably not. It's a big store and you get millions of customers."

"Yeah we did get a lot," she agreed. "Do you live far from here?"

"No, up the street."

"Show me where so I can pick you up later," said Kelli.

"You don't have to do that. I can meet you at the store."

"No. I get off at six, but sometimes I work later if it gets busy."

"All right," I said. "I'll show you my house."

We walked to Vodges Street in no time. I forgot about the steps until we were almost in front of the house. I cringed. I didn't want her to see them.

"Cathleen said she was going to get them fixed," I explained pointing to them.

"Don't worry about it," she dismissed it quickly.

"See you later," I said leaving her on the sidewalk as I ran up the crumbling stairs and into the house. I was excited. This was the first friend I had made around here. I needed one. I needed somebody to talk to. And it would mean getting out of that house more often.

"Thank you God," I whispered as I closed the front door.

CHAPTER SIX

I was standing at the top of the carpeted stairs when I heard the doorbell ring. I was brushing my teeth and the scent of peppermint clung to my lips. It's odor was strong, but pleasing to my nose. I was anxious to get to the door first so that was why I was cleaning my teeth in the hallway. I was all set to run for the front door, but Cathleen appeared from nowhere and answered it.

"Is Niara ready?"

"Niara? Do you know my daughter?" Cathleen asked eyeing the girl suspiciously. She looked like a girl Cathleen didn't want her daughter to associate with. The girl had a gold chain hanging from her neck and designer sunglasses on her nose. Everything she wore looked like it costed somebody some money. She had to be about sixteen. How did a girl her age dress like that? Maybe her parents had money, Cathleen consoled herself.

"I told her I'd be here at six."

"Are you sure you got the right house? My daughter doesn't know anybody around here."

"I got the right house. And she knows me."

"Who are you?"

"My name's Kelli. Is she here?"

"Where are you two supposed to be going?"

"Why don't you ask her?" the girl said not willing to volunteer any information.

"Because I'm asking you."

"Look I'm just here to pick her up. I'm not here to get

84

interrogated."

"Niara!" yelled Cathleen.

"I'm here," I said running quickly down the steps. I was anxious to get out of the house. And, I didn't want Cathleen getting in my business. "Hi Kelli. I'm ready."

"Ready for what? Who is this girl?"

"A friend."

"But you just met her. How can she be your friend?"

"How do you know who I know? It's not like you've been around me that long yourself."

"That's got nothing to do with this. I thought you were going to spend some time with Yvette and Sandra-- the girls across the street."

"Yes, you thought that. Anyway I got to go. Unless you are going to start picking my friends for me too."

"I'm not doing that, but they are nice girls. And I think you should meet them."

"Who wants to be around nice girls?" I mumbled. I wanted to reject everything she suggested.

"What did you say?" asked Cathleen.

"I said--" I wasn't allowed to finish repeating myself, because Kelli spoke up pretending to be insulted.

"Are you saying I'm not a nice girl?"

"I don't know. Are you?"

"Sometimes," said Kelli.

"I'm going," I said moving pass Cathleen. I grabbed Kelli's hand and we ran from the house before Cathleen could say anything more.

"What's up with your mom?" she asked rushing with me

down the cement steps.

"Who cares?" I said pulling my leather bag more securely over my shoulder.

"I thought she wasn't going to let you go."

"I'd like to see her stop me."

"Boy you really don't like her, do you?"

"Would you like a person who gave you away?"

"She did that?"

"Yes-- to my grandparents. Now she thinks she can just come back and everything will be all right. Well I don't want her in my life now. It's too late."

"That's deep," said Kelli. "Why did she do that?"

"I don't know. I guess she wanted her freedom-- probably didn't want to raise some kid."

"Sounds like you hate her."

"Wouldn't you?"

"I guess so."

"Then don't sound so surprised. I can't wait to get away from her."

As we walked down the street, I heard loud music coming from somebody's open car window. I allowed my head and shoulders to bop to the music. It was the number three top hit song, by a black British rapper. This was her second CD.

Kelli slowed up her walk so she could do a dance as we proceeded down the street. I looked at her and smiled. I hadn't noticed it before, but she was really pretty. She had her hair in microbraids. The hairstyle was a bob; it was the color of terra cotta. She had chinese eyes and thick lips. I wasn't sure how old she was and I guess it didn't matter.

As we continued down the street, I noticed a metallic red jeep approaching us. A boy stuck his head out of the passenger's window and shouted, "Work that body! Work that body! Make sure you don't hurt nobody!"

"I haven't done it yet," shouted Kelli. She let her hips and butt move to the music.

"Ahh girl you got it going on," he shouted back. "Sweet butt and a pretty face.

She smiled.

Was that a compliment? I didn't take it that way. I stopped dancing. I didn't like this kind of attention.

"You look kind of fine yourself," Kelli said.

Please don't let them stop. I didn't want to talk to them. They sounded rude, nasty.

The jeep drove off. And I gave up a sigh of relief.

"Do you know them?"

"No, but I'd like to. Too bad they didn't stop. It was two of them-- one for you and one for me."

"I'm not interested."

"That jeep was brand new."

"So what. I'm not impressed."

"Well I sure am. I'm tired of dealing with guys who ain't got nothing. Can't have fun with a broke brother. I don't care how hard you try. It just ain't happening."

"You are not really serious?" I asked.

"Yes I am. That's what my mom's always saying. Leave the ones with no money to themselves because they can't do nothing for nobody. I think she's right."

"I don't know about that. Right now I don't have any

money."

"That's different. You don't need money."

"Why not?"

"'cause the boy is supposed to take you out. He's supposed to pay for everything."

"Well just because a boy is broke that's not going to be the only reason why I won't talk to him."

"Say what you want, but I'm not going to be like that anymore. I'm tired of eating at fast food restaurants. And I'm tired of catching SEPTA to the movies-- no more. If he don't got a car, he can keep on walking."

"Do you have a boyfriend?" I wanted to know.

"No, but I'm looking. And I can tell you one thing, he sure enough ain't going to be from around here. Most of the ones around here don't have cars."

"Where are you looking?"

"In Mount Erie. That's where most of them--" she began, but she was interrupted by:

"Hey Kelli!" somebody was yelling from across the street. "Come here!"

We both looked to see who was doing the hollering. We saw a bunch of boys standing close together behind an iron wrought gate. It looked like they were at a swimming pool.

"What do you want?" yelled Kelli.

"Come here and see," he coaxed.

"Who's that with you?" someone else hollered.

"None of your business!" then she whispered to me. "They just want us to come over there so they can check you out. Do you want to go?"

"I don't care."

As we got closer to the boys, I counted four of them. They were all ordinary looking. None of them appealed to me, although, I could feel stares on my face and body. I remained quiet while Kelli did all the talking.

"So what do you want?" she asked.

"Why don't you come swimming with us?"

"Say what?"

"Take a dip in the pool."

"Do you see me wearing a bathing suit?"

"You don't' need one. What you got on is fine," he encouraged.

"I ain't getting into no dirty water with my clothes on. You must be kidding."

"Ah come on girl. It'll be fun."

"Yeah for you," she said looking behind him and into the swimming pool. "Where did you find them?"

Kelli was looking at two slightly fat girls jumping around in the water. One girl had on cut-off shorts and a tee-shirt with no bra. Her breast were jumping all over the place. She really looked nasty. It was hard to see what the other girl had on because she was surrounded by boys. Their hands were dunking and grabbing and pulling on her body. She was covered by hands. There was a lot of grinding and touching going on in that pool. And the girls seemed to be eating all the attention up.

"Why don't they just get a hotel room?" said Kelli, turning her eyes back to the boy who had called them over.

"It ain't like that. They just having a little fun."

"It looks like they're about to gang bang them to me," she

said.

"Damn! Your mind is in the gutter! Can't a boy have a little fun without being considered a dog?" he asked.

"Not when they are acting like that. And you think I'm going to climb this fence for that? No thank you."

"Don't hurt to ask-- who's your friend?"

"A friend," she said plainly.

"She got a name?"

"Ask her yourself."

"It's Niara," I said.

"You want to go swimming?" he was determined to get one of us in that pool.

"I can't swim."

"I can teach you."

"Awe quit it Jeff. You don't know how to swim yourself," joked one of the other boys.

"Then we can learn together," he said trying to coax me into agreeing.

"No thanks," I said.

"Are those coolers over there?" Kelli wanted to know.

Jeff nodded.

"Can I get one?"

"What will I get for it?"

"Go get me one first," she said.

"Okay," he walked away.

He came back in a matter of seconds. It took him even less time to climb the fence and hand her the coolers.

"Here's one for your friend too," he said grinning at me.

"Thanks," she said giving me one and opening hers. I held

on to mine. I didn't drink, but I felt uncomfortable saying it.

Jeff climbed back down the gate not taking his eyes off Kelli. The other boys standing at the gate began to drift back to the action in the pool. That left only Jeff talking to us.

"Nothing personal Niara, but can I talk to Kelli by herself for a minute," he asked.

"I don't care."

"Thanks," he said winking at me.

"I still ain't changing my mind. I'm not climbing no fence just to let some boy feel me up," she said as she followed Jeff further down the dividing fence.

She wasn't gone long before I heard Kelli wandering back over to me, "He didn't want nothing-- still trying to talk me into climbing that fence."

"I guess he failed."

"Yeah," she said and then. "I think somebody is checking you out real hard," she spoke into my ear.

"Who?" I asked casually.

"Him. Over there in the white trunks. Damn! He's good-looking-- and he's got a body," she whispered even closer into my ear.

"I don't see him-- oh," I said focusing on a black boy at the other side of the pool. One glance caused me to look away from him in embarrassment. He was wearing skimpy trunks that showed off way too much, and he definitely was staring at somebody.

"Is he happening or what?"

"He looks okay I guess," but the trimmer in my voice was betraying the words I spoke.

"You guess? Girl you don't have to guess. I'm telling you he is."

"How do you know it's me he's staring at?"

"Because I saw him watching you when I was back there talking to Jeff."

"I don't believe you," I said remembering the trick she played on me this morning in the park.

"I know what I'm talking about. He's on you."

"So what if he is? I'm not interested in meeting anyone," I said averting my eyes even further from where he stood.

"Are you sure? He looks like somebody I'd like to get to know. He's got money too. I've seen his car. It's new."

I ignored Kelli's comments; I didn't care if he had money or not. I stole another look at him. He must be about 6'4"; he was solid. Smooth muscles and tight brown skin covered every part of his body my eyes hit. He must lift weights. He had a close hair cut. Adorning his long, brown neck was a black, white, and yellow wooden necklace. It hugged his neck.

"Niara he's walking this way!"

"No he's not," I said looking up just to make sure she wasn't telling the truth. I immediately felt sweat gripping my arm pits. I looked down at the ground quickly. He was coming this way. But that didn't mean he was going to walk over here. Maybe he was leaving.

"But he didn't do that. He stopped right in front of the silver fence-- right in front of me.

"What's your name?" he asked eliminating any preliminary custom of working up to asking a stranger's name.

"Niara," I was nervous. The word was a whisper.

92

"Niara you are one of the finest looking girls I've ever seen," he said in a smooth slow voice. It was very sexy and very baritoned. His eyes took in my face, my eyes, my very young and straight body.

"My name's Ty."

I stared at him. He was completely good-looking up close, but his words turned me off. He was using a line on me.

"Is this your friend?" he asked, referring to Kelli.

"Does it matter?"

"I wouldn't have asked if it didn't," he remarked.

"I thought it was another one of your lines."

"What did you say?"

"Ah cut it out Niara," the other girl interrupted. "Don't be so cold. I'm Kelli."

I ignored her, "I said try your lines on somebody else."

He looked taken aback by my words. I don't know if I said what I did because I thought he was cute and I wanted more than a line from him. Why was I challenging him? Was I hoping he did think I was attractive and did want more than just a few hours of flirtation. I don't know why I did it.

"I don't use lines. I don't need them."

"That's what it sounded like to me."

"Look, maybe this is all a mistake. I don't begin relationships with arguments. If I'd known you'd be this hostile, I would not have wasted my time," he said and then walked away.

"I don't believe you! You just brushed him off like that!"

"That's what he deserved."

"I know you thought he was cute. So why did you do that?"

93

"Because he wasn't being himself."

"As good as he looks, he ain't got to be himself. He can be whoever he wants to be."

"Not to me. I've had enough of people like that-- I can't trust somebody who's phony."

"Listen to you. I thought you wasn't interested in getting a boyfriend."

"I'm not, but if I was I'd want him to be genuine."

"Ohhh listen to the girl-- genuine," she mimicked. "That's the only thing she's interested in."

"Oh shut up," I said, playfully shoving her. "Do you feel like walking me to Turner's. I want a soda and some chips," I was trying to divert her attention away from me.

"Don't you want that cooler?"

"No."

"Can I have it?"

"No," I said handing it to her playfully.

CHAPTER SEVEN

I don't believe in fate or destiny or any of that psychic stuff, but there must be some reason why I keep running into him. I'm talking about Ty. No matter where I am, he seems to pop up. It's been a week since I met him at the pool and I've run into him three times already.

The first time we met I was standing in line at the local drug store. I needed to buy panty-shields. It was a habit Grandmother got me into every since I got my first period.

I couldn't buy them at Turner's; I would've been too embarrassed so I walked four blocks to this store.

I was standing in this slow moving line, checking out all the magazine covers. They were all glossy, waterproof covers showing off beautiful models wearing sexy, tight clothes that I did not have the nerve to put on.

I compared their perfect white features to my own and felt inadequate. I had long black hair, but it was not as long as theirs or as straight. I had green eyes, but they were not a deep silvery blue like the slender girl looking up at me from the rack. My nose was small, but distinctly a black feature. And our bodies had absolutely nothing in common. Mine was skinny and flat chested, while her body was curvy with big breast.

All the comparing I did was on a subconscious level and if someone had verbally said these things to me I would have denied them. I would have denied being programmed by a larger society into believing that the perfect features were the pale, white features.

As I continued to look at the magazine model, I heard a voice speaking into my ear, "Niara?"

It was a deep and familiar voice.

I turned around abruptly to stare into a warm pair of brown eyes.

"Ahh-- hi," I said immediately grabbing a magazine and shoving it into my basket. I hoped it was big enough to hide the box of panty-shields that seemed to have grown instantaneously. I shifted the box and magazine several different ways. Was it completely covered? Or could he see the pink corners trying to peek out? I felt hot flashes hit my face as I tried to keep the box from his view. He seemed not to notice.

"I didn't think I'd be seeing you again," he smiled. "Are you still angry with me?"

"For what?" I said trying to appear nonchalant. I didn't think it was working.

"You tell me. You were the one acting hostile."

"I was not," I defended. "And no I'm not mad at you."

"Good-- do you live 'round here?" he asked changing the focus of the conversation.

"Ahhh-- yes. On Vodges Street."

"When did you move there?"

"How do you know I haven't been there all my life?"

"Now who's playing games?" he asked.

"Okay," I admitted. "I moved there two weeks ago," I continued staring at him.

Today he was fully dressed. He was wearing tight black biker shorts and a white tee-shirt. I nervously glanced away from his eyes; I looked down at his feet. He was wearing white

96

sneakers. They looked like he had just taken them out of the box. I looked back up and into his face. He was giving me a deepening smile and it continued to grow as I shyly examined him. He still wore the African necklace, but today he also wore a linked gold chain. He was carrying a white helmet in his left hand and some lottery tickets in the other.

"You play?" I asked. After I did so, I wondered how I could ask such a silly question. Of course he played, if he was holding the tickets in his hand.

"Only if I get a feeling about the number. You?"

"No. I can't afford it."

"Why not?"

"No job."

"Don't you got a boyfriend?"

"No," I said happy to give him this bit of information. "But if I did, I wouldn't be taking his money. I want my own."

"If you were mine, you'd take it."

"Why?"

"Because if I gave it to you, that means I want you to have it-- do you got a lucky number?"

I started to ask why, but I didn't feel confident enough. All the words I spoke kept getting caught in my throat, so I said as little as possible.

"2557," I made the numbers sound like one word.

"You got a four digit lucky number?" he smiled not believing me.

I wanted to say it's the last four digits to my phone number, but my voice failed me and all I could say was, "Yes."

He looked at me strangely, "You sure it's not a Mac card

number or something else?"

"It's just four numbers."

"Do you want them boxed or straight?"

"Huh?"

"The numbers. Box them or play them straight?"

"I don't know."

"I'll do both," he said.

And without saying anything else, he walked away leaving me and a few other women who'd gotten in line after me to stare at his retreating body.

One woman asked me boldly, "Is that your boyfriend?"

I was surprised by the question, but answered it out of instinct.

"No-- I just met him."

"Then leave him alone-- leave him alone before you get your feelings hurt. He's too good-looking to be any good. He'll use you right on up and then toss you aside. I know what I'm talking about. I've had too many do it to me not to recognize the type," she said trying to offer me a bit of advise; I assumed. But why should I listen to her? What did she know about Ty or me?

I looked at her. I guess my expression showed what I was thinking because she said, "You think I'm crazy, don't you? But I've been around a lot longer than you. And I've seen and felt things I hope you never do," she said in a serious tone.

I said nothing.

"I'm just trying to warn you. He ain't about nothing. He might be good for sex, but that's it. He won't be around for long after that."

Sex? What was she talking about? I wasn't thinking about

that. Why was she saying this stuff to me? I was just thinking he was cute-- that's all.

"I'm not going to have sex with him."

"You're not? If that's the case, you better keep on walking 'cause he is going to want that. Trust me."

I dismissed her as a nut and looked for Ty. He was taller than I first thought-- and gorgeous too. I noticed this as he walked back to me.

"Here," he said handing me the tickets. "If you win, you gotta take me out."

"And if you win?" I asked.

"Then I'm gonna have a surprise for you. I played 5055," he said.

I did not say a word, but I engraved the numbers in my head.

"What kind of surprise?" I was intrigued. I felt like he was flirting with me, but he didn't say anything to prove it.

"You'll have to close your eyes tight and see."

"Like this?" I said playfully closing my eyes and smiling.

"Now make a wish,' he said seriously.

"Okay," I said with my eyes still closed. "I want a--"

I stopped speaking when I felt his lips brush against mine. It wasn't a kiss, because I barely felt the touch. I felt his breathe more than his lips.

My eyes popped open. I stared into his laughing brown ones, "Surprise."

I didn't move away. I didn't notice the women behind me

whispering. I didn't notice anything.

"I-- am," I stammered. I couldn't look away.

"Your eyes are beautiful. They are so wide. They look like they are going to jump out of your head-- wide and innocent. Haven't you been kissed before?"

"No," I said truthfully.

"Somebody's going to have a lot of fun teaching you," he said backing away from me.

"Is-- that going to be my surprise?"

"No," he said in a low tone. "Don't look disappointed."

"I'm not!" I said not wanting him to think I wanted him to do that to me.

"We'll see," he said.

"If-- you win, how will I get my surprise?" I tried to lick the dryness away from my lips as I spoke. "You don't know where I live."

"I can find your house. I already know the street."

"No! Don't do that," I said reality sinking in. Cathleen wasn't going to let him take me out. She would go off the deep end if he came to the house looking for me.

"Why not?"

"I'd just rather wait. That's all."

He didn't press me for a reason, but said, "Then you'll have to call me. My number's on the back of the ticket."

I immediately flipped the tickets over and spotted it.

For the first time I wondered how old he was. I could certainly tell he wasn't my age. He didn't look old, but there was no way that he was eighteen or nineteen. He was out of his teens.

"How old are you?" I blurted out awkwardly. Now I had

just asked him a second silly question. I was on a roll today. He didn't think age was a problem so why was I acting like it was a big deal? I probably seemed childish to him with all these goofy questions.

"Twenty-three. Is that too old for you?"

"Ahhh no. I was just wondering."

"You don't like older men?" he asked an intense expression crossed his face. It caused his thick, bushy eyebrows to draw together.

"It depends on the person," I said trying to sound older than sixteen.

"Good. I feel the same."

"I hope you win," I said not knowing what else to say.

"So do I," he smiled implying much with those three words. "I got to go," he said. "I didn't lock my bike up outside."

"Okay," I said and watched him walk pass the register and out the door.

If the line I was standing in moved, I sure wasn't aware of it. All I could think of was how nice I was feeling. He could make living in Philadelphia very, very exciting. I unloaded my basket onto the counter. The cashier told me how much the bill was, but I didn't hear her. She gave me my change. I bagged the magazine I hadn't intended to buy, and the other stuff. I walked through the sliding double door and out into a sunny day.

That evening I broke another one of my promises. The first one was using her water to take a bath. And now I was turning on Cathleen's television at seven o'clock. I had to watch the lottery. I had to know if he won. I didn't think I was going to win. After all, how lucky could Cathleen's phone number be?

101

Neither of us hit the number that night, but I felt a special bond knowing that we were both watching it at the same time. I know that sounds corny, but so what. It's how I feel. And nobody knows how I feel, but me. I wanted to call him, but I didn't have the nerve. What would we talk about? I had no idea, so I hid the tickets and his phone number under the rug in my room. I didn't want Cathleen to find it just in case she went snooping through my stuff.

Don't get me wrong. I wanted to call him. I even went as far as dialing his number a couple of times, but I always ended up slamming the phone down just before someone answered it.

CHAPTER EIGHT

One.

Two.

Three.

Four. I drank four glasses of lukewarm, tap water and it didn't help. I was still hungry. I wanted to go downstairs and open the refrigerator door and eat everything on the shelves. I was starving? I hadn't eaten food in two days! No hoagies. No onion rings. No potato chips. No grape sodas-- just cloudy glasses of tap water. I ran out of money and I refused to eat her food.

I didn't feel good. I could feel myself getting dizzier. I sank to the floor in the bathroom and cried. I wasn't going to be able to continue drinking water, but I didn't want her food. I didn't want to need her for anything. But as I was thinking this, I knew I was going to break another one of my promises. I hated it. She was going to win. This was her house, her food, and her money. I wanted to defy her. I had to. I got up from the floor. I tried to drink one more glass of water. Maybe the hunger would go away. I put the thin glass to my lips. I took one sip and spit the nasty liquid out. I couldn't do it. I had to get something to eat.

I left the bathroom quietly and gingerly walked down the stairs. I made it to the kitchen without too much noise.

What should I eat? I opened cabinet door after cabinet door searching for food. I didn't see anything I wanted. I then moved to the refrigerator. There was bacon, sausage, milk, eggs, orange juice... I took out the eggs, milk, bacon, butter, cheese-- I drank a cup of juice. It went down fast. I could hear it sloshing around in my stomach. It combined with the four cups of water I had already drank. Was I going to vomit? I crossed my fingers and waited. Nothing happened.

This was going to be one gigantic breakfast. I was not going to be hungry again for days. I took a bowl from the cabinet and began cracking my eggs just like Grandmother used to do. I thought sadly about her being gone. There wasn't a day that I didn't think about her or miss her.

I turned on the radio. It was sitting on the windowsill. The sound was so low it barely filled that area of the kitchen. I didn't want to wake Cathleen. I didn't want her to know I needed her. Let her think I was starving. Let her worry if she was capable of that.

I was standing over the black skillet pan turning strip after strip of red-brown bacon-- the grease was splattering everywhere when Cathleen quietly walked into the kitchen.

I froze.

I was caught.

All I could do was stand there and stare at her.

"Kind of late for breakfast," she said surveying the eggshells on the counter.

"I got hungry," I mumbled.

"I can see," she said, her eyes laughing at my predicament. "It looks like you're cooking for three people-- what happened? You got tired of all that delicious water? I thought you were going to turn into a fish," she said walking to the counter. Cathleen began clearing some of the garbage away.

"I like water," I mumbled.

"Ohhh. So this food isn't for you?"

"Yes it is," I answered quickly. I responded as though I thought she was going to snatch the food away from me.

"Couldn't keep up the hunger strike-- them stomach pains started kicking you in the butt, huh?"

She was laughing at me again.

I said nothing, but smiled guiltily.

"You did good. Most people wouldn't have made it the first day. You made it two whole days. Congratulations."

Was that a compliment? Was she giving me a show of respect? I wanted to believe it. It would help me accept my defeat so I took it that way. Now I didn't feel entirely bad about getting caught.

Cathleen moved about the kitchen getting out glasses and napkins and forks and knives. She acted like she was preparing the table for some elaborate guess. She set the table for two people.

"Arc you cating too?" I askcd.

"I thought you might need some help. That's too much food for one person."

"Is it?"

"Don't tell me you are going to be selfish-- didn't anyone teach you about sharing? Most sixteen-year-old girls can't eat six eggs. Or-- one, two, three, four pieces of toast and six strips of bacon."

"I wanted to make sure there was enough," I said lamely.

"You definitely got that and more."

"Do you like garlic? I put some in the eggs."

"I don't know. But it smells good."

105

I began serving the eggs onto the plates. As I did so, I could hear her pouring the juice.

"Who did the cooking at your house?" she asked awkwardly.

"Me."

"How long have you been doing it?"

"Since I was eight," I said, handing her a plate and putting mine down in front of me.

"Eight? What did you cook at eight?"

"Simple stuff," I reached for the strawberry preserves. "Grandmah even taught me how to make stuff like this," I said proudly. I spread some on my slice of toast.

"You can make strawberry preserves?" she asked in amazement.

"It's not hard."

"I'm impressed."

"Don't be, anybody can do it," I said taking a bite of toast. "I'll make you some if you want."

"Would you?" she said shocked by my offer. "I'd like that."

"You'd better eat or your food is going to get cold," I warned.

CHAPTER NINE

Kelli and I have absolutely nothing in common. She likes apples; I can't stand them. I hate trying to chew up the waxy, thick skin that protects the inside of every one I've ever bitten into. And she loves their skin. Every time she comes to my house, she is munching on one-- devouring it like it was candy.

Even when it comes to clothes, we don't match up. She likes mini-skirts and I won't wear them. I refused to show off my skinny, pale legs, but she reveled in showing hers off. Maybe if I had shapely ones like Kelli's I'd feel a little differently. But I don't, so I prefer to be seen in blue jeans and loafers.

I like reading black poetry, especially anything written by Naomi Long Madget. But Kelli won't read any poetry to save her life. I tried once to give her my favorite book, BLACK VOICES, but she skillfully left it at my house when she went home.

But for two people so different as we are, I find myself spending a lot of time with her. We are becoming very close. I like her attitude. She doesn't care what anybody thinks about her including Cathleen.

Cathleen hasn't come out and said anything to me, but I know she doesn't like Kelli. I know Kelli is aware of it too. I'm not sure why Cathleen feels this way, but I really don't care. That's her problem, not mine. I think she is afraid to say anything negative to me. She is trying to keep things civil in the house. It's been a week since we ate breakfast together and the arguments were not so intense anymore. They were about little things like who was going to clean the kitchen or who used the iron last and forgot to turn it off.

"Why do you always buy that color lipstick?" I asked from the bed in my so called room.

"'cause I like it," said Kelli, looking at me like that was a silly question for me to ask.

"I think you'd look better without it."

"I don't. Purple brings my face out. You should try wearing some. I bet orange would look good on you."

"Nah," I said. "I don't like that thick gook on my mouth."

"Fine," she said continuing to cake purple plum on her lips.

"What time are you supposed to be at Turner's?"

"Two o'clock."

I looked at the digital. She had only twenty minutes, "Do you want me to walk you there?"

"If you want."

"I don't have anything else to do," I said getting up from the bed. I grabbed my keys and we left.

We reached Turner's mini-market after crossing a series of streets and traffic lights. People were everywhere: on their porches, on cemented steps, hanging on corners, lounging in cars, some were in the middle of the street playing dodge-ball. And they were all doing the same things, communicating and laughing and enjoying the wariness of the summer day.

Kelli entered the mini-market followed by me. Instant, startling blindness engulfed us as; we stepped through the doorway. The lighting in the store was nowhere near as powerful as that of the sun. The sudden change in lighting caused my eyes darted from place to place trying to adjust. When they did focus, it was on Mr. Turner. He was behind the deli waiting on a little boy. "Hi Mr. Turner," said Kelli. "Hi Kelli. I see you brought help. Hi Niara. Are you working again today?" he teased, because I always hung around his storc hclping Kclli stock thc shclvcs or count mcrchandisc. Whatever she happened to be doing at the time.

"Yes," I said.

"You want me to finish stamping the prices on these cans?" asked Kelli.

"That's a good idea. You can do that," he agreed.

"What can I do?" I asked.

"I'm going to start feeling guilty Niara. You've been helping out here so much. Pretty soon I'm going to have to put you on the payroll-- instead of giving you hoagies and sodas."

"You should," broke in Kelli. "She's always complaining about how broke she is. I'm getting tired of hearing it."

"No Mr. Turner. You don't have to feel like that. I like hanging around here," I said picking up a can of corn Kelli had just priced and placing it on the shelf.

"As much business as we do Mr. Turner, I think you need somebody like Niara working here. She won't be as good as me," Kelli smiled at me. "But she could help out a lot. You know, sweep up, mop the floors, clean out the freezers and stock the diary products. It gets real cold in there and somebody's got to do it..."

"It sounds like you want me to do all the dirty stuff," I whispered to Kelli.

"I do," she agreed.

"That's not fair."

"Yes it is. I was here first," she said to Mr. Turner, "So what do you say? Are you going to give her a job?"

"I don't know. Do you want one Niara?"

"Do I want one? Yes! Definitely!"

"Then I think we can arrange something. But, I need to talk to your mother first to get her approval."

"Why does she need to know?"

"Because you are under age. And she should know where you are."

"If you have to," I said reluctantly.

I didn't understand how in one year a woman who did absolutely nothing for me my whole entire life was suddenly the person making all the important decisions for me. She could determine where I lived, what I ate, and now whether or not I worked in this store.

"Is she at home right now?" he asked.

"I guess so. She doesn't go to work until four."

"What's your telephone number?"

"729-2557."

"Kelli ring this little fellow up for a pound of American cheese, a half a pound of smoked ham, and a half a pound of bologna. I'll be right back."

"Don't you want to know what her name is?" I asked.

"I already know it."

"How?"

"She came in here one day looking for you," he said disappearing into the back of the store.

"She did?"

"You don't think she'd say no, do you?" asked Kelli.

"Probably," I said unhappily. "She'd just love to show me who's the adult and who's the child."

"I hope not. I want you to work here."

"So do I, but you can forget it now," I said as Mr. Turner walked back into our sights.

"So what did she say?" I asked.

"Guess," he said.

"No," I stated.

"Are you sure?"

"Yes."

"Then it seems to me you don't know your mother very well."

"She said yes!" I demanded excitedly.

"She did."

"I don't believe it," I said.

"Ask her for yourself when you get home," he said handing me an apron identical to the one Kelli was wearing.

CHAPTER TEN

1. Across. Nearsighted cartoon character? Fearless fly? I began spelling the word out. F E A R L. No, too many letters. Mr. Magoo? M R. M A G O O. No, that didn't fit either. What about just M A G O O? It fit! I scribbled the letters into the appropriate boxes and read another question.

13. Down. Birds beak? Bill? No, it had to be three letters. I already had the first two. N I. What was the last letter? I didn't know. Nig? Nit? Ni_ what? I'd come back to that one.

I looked at a few other questions; they looked equally as hard as 13. Down.

14. Across. Exclude socially? O _ _ R A _ _ _ E? Huh? I has no idea. What about 1. Down? Unjoined projecting appendages (octopus). Tentacles? T E N T A C L E S. It fit!

$$
\begin{array}{l}
\text{T} \\
\text{E} \\
\text{N} \\
\text{T} \\
\text{A} \\
\text{C} \\
\text{L} \\
\text{E} \\
\text{OS\_RA\_ \_ \_ E}
\end{array}
$$

Exclude socially?
O S _ R A _ _ _ E?
Ostracize! That had to be it! I marked in the letters.

They fit.

I was about to go to the next question, but an old woman started unloading her plastic basket of groceries in front of me. I turned the crossword book face-down with the pages open and began ringing up her stuff. Eggs. Bacon. Tuna fish. Bread. Apples (I made a nasty face). Spaghetti. Tomato paste. Mozzarella cheese...

"$25.47," I said.

She gave me her money. Two tens and two fives.

"$4.53," I said handing her the change.

I bagged her purchases and wished her a nice day.

The next person in my line was Ty! The last time I saw him he was talking to someone on a pay phone. But, he didn't see me.

Right now, he was holding a sandwich in his hand. It was probably made by Kelli. She was working in the deli. I looked toward her work section, but she was busy making another sandwich. I looked again at Ty. He put the sandwich, a bag of chips, and a two liter soda on the counter.

"Hi," I said demurely. I was too, too nervous. I didn't know what to do or say. I began to ring up his order.

He nodded his head, acknowledging my greeting; and then abruptly asked, "Why didn't you call me?"

"Because I didn't win," I said, but he didn't appreciate my joke. "It's Seven dollars and fifty-one cents," I said awkwardly.

He pulled out a twenty; and, I reached for it.

"You didn't answer my question," he said staring at me.

"I don't know," I said lamely. I couldn't tell him the truth. I couldn't tell him that the reason I didn't call was because I was

113

scared.

"You said you didn't like lines or games, right?"

"Yes," I admitted. I didn't like the way this was going. I was beginning to feel trapped by my own words.

"I don't like games either," he said.

I didn't speak, but I watched him closely.

"So I'm telling you point blank so there are no misunderstandings. I want to go out with you-- get to know you."

"You do?" I couldn't believe my ears.

"Yes."

"When?"

"Tonight. After you get off."

"I can't."

"Why not?" he seemed irritated.

"It'll be too late when I get off."

"What time is that?"

"Nine."

"That's not late," he said.

"It is to Cathleen."

"Who?"

"My mother."

"Don't tell me you're one of those girls who has to follow a curfew."

"What's that supposed to mean?"

"That you must let your mother run your life. Is that how it is?"

"Not for me, but I'm not going nowhere with somebody I don't know. Not at night."

"Are you scared?"

114

"No.   Just smart enough not to get into that kind of situation."

"Fair enough," he said.   "But next time I ask you out, I don't want to hear no."

"If it's at night--"

"I got the message," he said.

"Good," I said.   I thought he had forgotten about me after all this time.

"Now put my stuff in a bag so I can go."

"Here's your change," I said reaching out to him.

"Keep it."

"I can't take your money--"

"It's a tip," he said walking to the door.

A tip?   Nobody leaves $12.49 as a tip.   Was he trying to impress me?   Did he think he could buy me?   What was I getting myself into?   I looked at the money.   I wasn't sure what to do with it.   Should I keep it?   I could buy Marietta Brown's latest book of poetry or I could put some money to it and buy a new pair of loafers.   The ones I had on right now were dogged.   I thought about it for a minute.   Grandmother had warned my about taking money from a boy.   She said this could lead to misunderstandings.   He might think he is entitled to something that he is not.   So to avoid problems Grandmother always advised me against it.   I opened the cash register and deposited the bills into the appropriate spaces.   I let the change rattle in their individual compartments and then closed the draw.   I didn't feel right about accepting his money.   I would tell Mr. Turner about it.

CHAPTER ELEVEN

"Did you grow up around here Mr. Turner?"

"Yes. I've been here all my life."

"Have you ever met my mother? I mean do you know anything about her? Why she got into drugs? How she could just throw her life away like that?"

Lately I've been thinking a lot about Cathleen. I've been trying to figure out why she made the choices she did. How she got hooked on heroin.

This whole train of thinking stemmed from me finding a picture lying in the bottom of a storage draw in the kitchen. I was looking for a pencil to complete the crossword puzzle I got from the Sunday paper. I was bored and needed something to do. I was off and Cathleen had already left for work. She wouldn't be back until twelve; she worked the second shift at C. R. Drew Hospital.

It didn't really matter to me what time she went to work or when she got off. We rarely talked or seemed to have any of the same interest. It's just that her absence made the house more unbearable. When she was gone, the house became inactive. The phone seldom rang unless it was Kelli calling; the radio was quiet, and the place didn't smell of her cooking which was almost as good as mine.

So I used the excuse of needing a pencil to go looking through her stuff. And that's how I found the picture. It was a picture of five girls. They were bunched together and smiling. It appeared to be a picture taken at a photo booth. They were falling all over themselves in an attempt to fit into the camera shot. Cathleen was one of the girls. She looked extremely happy. And she didn't look like someone who needed drugs. So why? What happened? And she was so pretty. I studied the picture for a long time before finally putting it into my pocket. For some reason I wanted to keep it.

Mr. Turner began to speak, "I knew your mother. She was a lot younger than me, but I saw her around."

"So what was she like-- what happened to her?"

"Too many things."

"Like?"

"Like the same things that happen to too many black kids-- she had a mother who wasn't around because she was always working. And when she did get time off, she wanted to spend it with her male friends instead of her children. Cathleen's father never came through here to see her."

"I know how that is," I said.

"So did she. It's a shame too. The only thing Cathleen knows about her father is his name and when he was murdered," said Mr. Turner.

"He got killed?"

"Don't nobody know who did it. It happened somewhere in New York."

"How old was she then?"

"I think she must have been eleven."

"She was?"

"I believe so."

"What about school? Did she like it?"

"I don't know. She never really finished school. I tried to

convince her, but she got pregnant and that was that-- her mind just wasn't on school."

"Did you know my father too?"

"Never met him, but I'd seen him around. I think he had some family living here. Somehow they met and hooked up one summer."

"I guess they didn't love each other?"

"Not the way I see it. After that summer, I didn't see him around the neighborhood again-- the next thing I know, Cathleen is walking around showing you off. Telling everybody your name is Niara."

"She did?"

"She did," he stated. "You were a beautiful, fat baby-- all cheeks and big green eyes. And she was so proud of you."

"So you knew who I was before I told you my name? 'Isn't your name Swahili?' I said mimicking him.

"Yes I did. Not too many girls with that name," he teased. "But I couldn't tell you that. If you thought I knew your mother, you probably would have become tight lipped."

"You got that right. I would not have told you a thing. But I still can't believe you . I thought adults didn't lie," I teased.

"We don't. We just don't always admit everything we know."

"I see."

"I don't know how she chose that name, but it suits you. It was your destiny to come back to your mother. She needs somebody to love her. She's had very little of it in her life."

"What about her mother? Was she mad when she found out Cathleen was pregnant with me?"

"She didn't show it. I guess she expected it to happen. She seemed to tolerate it until Cathleen moved out."

"Is that why Cathleen turned to drugs? Because she had a rough life?"

"I don't know why she did what she did. I can only say things were not easy for her. She was poor-- had no real education-- she had no job and the only friends she had were into that life style. So she went that way."

"But she knew you, didn't she?"

"Yes, but I was not one of her peers. We only knew each other causally-- mostly by sight. We sometimes talked when I saw her on the street."

"Oh," I said.

"Did you know she let my grandparents raise me?"

"Somebody told me that. I wasn't surprised. She was too young for a baby."

"I was three when it happened."

"The whole affair was a sad thing. Maybe giving you to your grandparents was the best thing at the time."

"But she's my mother. I should have been with her."

"Not if the only thing she could teach you was how to be like her."

"But I wanted to be with her."

"She did what she thought was right. What can I say? How are the two of you getting along?"

Now it was his turn to quiz me. He waited for my answer.

"Okay, I guess. We don't talk that much, but we have stopped arguing.

"That's a good sign."

119

"Maybe," I commented.

"Give her a chance Niara. It wasn't easy for her to quit drugs. Too many people can't seem to do it."

"Did she do it for me?" I asked needing an easy reason to forgive her. I could not simply do it unselfishly. If she did it for me, that would make my forgiving her justifiable.

"You got to do it for yourself. Doing it for somebody else doesn't work. Ask her about it if you want to know."

"Maybe I will."

CHAPTER TWELVE

I could not bring myself to ask Cathleen why she started using that stuff or why she stopped. I thought about all the whys, but did not feel comfortable enough to ask her.

If she wanted to tell me anything, I would let her volunteer it. I was not forgiving her for any of the pain I experienced growing up without her, but I decided not to hold it against her either. I wanted to just begin our relationship from this point.

An attempt to show this decision was expressed when I decided to cook Monday's dinner while Cathleen was at work.

"And what's that supposed to be?" Kelli asked looking over my shoulder and into the pot of frying meat on the stove.

"It is catfish," I said sarcastically. "Don't you have eyes."

"Don't look like fish to me. Does she like this kind of food?" Kelli asked screwing up her nose and grimacing. She surveyed the ingredients covering the countertops.

"I guess so. She cut out this recipe and put it in her cookbook," I said.

"Catfish and corn chowder? I know I said I would stay for dinner, but Niara! I don't know if I'm going to be able to hang with that stuff. Fish soup? My idea of dinner is not wet fish."

"It doesn't smell too bad," I tried to entice her.

"You can go ahead and believe that if you want to. But I don't like what I'm smelling."

"That's because the only thing you eat are cheese-steak hoagies."

"At least I can say it taste good."

"This will too-- I thought you were coming over here to help me?"

"You didn't tell me on the phone that you were making this," said Kelli.

"So what. You can start cutting up the onions," I pointed to them. "I need one full cup."

"Where's the recipe? I want to see it," said Kelli.

"Here," I handed it to her.

"You need all this for soup?" she said scanning the paper clipping.

"Come on Kelli. I don't need a critic. After you do the onions, I need--"

"I can read," said Kelli putting the paper down and getting to work.

It didn't take that long to prepare the soup or the homemade rye bread. We started the meal at eleven so that it would be fresh when Cathleen got home.

Kelli set the table and helped me clean up the kitchen. When I heard the front door open, I felt a little nervous grumbling in my stomach.

Was she going to understand what I was trying to say? Was she going to accept it after all the mean and hurtful things I had said to her? I had no way of knowing so I waited--

"Surprise!" emitted Kelli.

"I see," said Cathleen putting down her bag. "What's all this for?" she inquired looking at me.

"I thought I'd cook dinner for a change. No big deal."

"I see. It smells really good. What it is?"

"Go wash your hands and see," I said.

She did what I said, but I barely heard the water in the kitchen turn on and off before she was walking back into the dining room and pulling out a chair.

All the food was laid out on the table so Kelli and I seated ourselves also.

"What is it?" Cathleen repeated.

"Guess," I encouraged.

"It doesn't smell like anything I've had before."

"I know it ain't nothing I've had before," said Kelli making a face and then smiling self-consciously.

"Taste it." I said.

"I really didn't expect this," she said dishing out some of the soup and spilling it into her bowl.

"Yeah, you go first," Kelli added.

"Haven't you tried it yet?" she asked stopping the spoon at her lips.

"No!" said Kelli. "We made it for you. So you try it first."

"I don't know if I like that," said Cathleen slowly bringing the spoon closer to her mouth. She tasted it gingerly.

"And?" I asked waiting for a response.

"And I'm not saying a word. This test rat isn't talking. If you want to know, try tasting it for yourselves," she said putting the spoon down.

"Oh that's not right," I said. "We made it."

"And you should've tested it too."

"Your turn Niara," said Kelli.

"I have no problem with eating it," I said stuffing a spoonful into my mouth so fast it would make a fly blink.

"Now you," said Cathleen looking at Kelli.

"All right, all right," she said tasting her soup equally as fast as I did.

"It tastes okay," said Kelli.

"It tastes like catfish," said Cathleen. "Did you use the recipe I got out of the Sunday paper?"

"I found it in your cookbook."

"That's the one," she informed us. "When I cut it out, I wasn't sure if I was going to like it. You did a good job," she complimented.

"Thanks."

"What about me? I did some of the work too," said Kelli.

"Yeah, she cut up the onions and complained."

"See if I help you again."

"You both did a good job," Cathleen smiled. She was happy to spread the compliments around.

"Does this mean you two will be cooking more often?"

"Not me. Cooking ain't my thing," said Kelli.

"Maybe," I said.

After we ate dinner, Cathleen suggested that we walk down to the local ice cream parlor. She bought me a frozen yogurt topped with strawberries, chocolate chips, bananas, honey, wheat germ, and wet walnuts.

Kelli wanted a pint of chocolate-chocolate ice cream; she also got wet walnuts on top and Cathleen settled for vanilla bean ice cream on a sugar cone.

This was the first time I really liked being around her.

I caught it. This one looked like it might cover my stomach. It was black and made out of a stretchable material. "I like it," I said holding it up against a pair of blue jeans.

"Then go try it on," she yelled.

"Don't get pushy," I said feeling just a little excited. Ty asked me out; and, this was going to be my first date. I just didn't feel right wearing my old clothes. I wanted something new. And kind of sexy. So that's what all this was about. First new clothes and then Kelli promised to do something about my hair. I rushed into the fitting room with the clothes draped over my arm. I also carried a pair of black mules. I stripped in no time. I looked at myself in the mirror and realized how unusual I was. I think I'm the only girl in America who still wears a bra, panties and an undershirt. I was 16 and still dressed the way my Grandmother told me to. I peeled off the undershirt and felt a little odd. I felt like I was disobeying her. But I didn't stop, I took off the bra and feeling embarrassed quickly slid on the halter top. I wasn't ashamed of my breast. Only of the fact that I knew my Grandmother wouldn't like this top. It was definitely too tight. You could see every curve in my breast. I tried to pull it down to cover my stomach, but the halter kept creeping up until it rested just about my navel. I gave up trying to hide it and stepped into the blue jeans. Unlike the top, they were loose and hung down to my waist. I'd have to get a belt, I thought. I anxiously pulled off my loafers and socks. I couldn't wait to see how I looked in the mules. They would be the first pair of high-heeled shoes I owned. I delicately put them on. I then glanced at myself in the mirror. I was surprised at the person looking back at me. I no longer looked 16. I looked older. I looked like a woman-- except for my hair. It was pulled back in a ponytail. But my body! It didn't look like it belonged to me. My breast looked bigger under the black top. And, the heels gave me much height. I couldn't do anything but stare at my image.

"Are you ever coming out?" yelled Kelli.

"Uh-- right now."

"Sooo-- do it," she encouraged.

I stepped out and felt more embarrassed. I quickly looked around the store to see if it was still empty. I let out a sound of relief. Only Kelli was in the store.

"What do you think?" I asked.

"I'm jealous," she teased. "You ain't gonna leave a man for nobody else around here," but she winked at me and I knew she was just playing.

"Maybe I could find a bigger top," I said tugging at the bottom of the halter. It would not relinquish its position. It still rested just above my navel.

"No!" It's you and you're getting it," insisted Kelli. "And it don't look sleazy," she said sarcastically. Okay?"

I looked at myself in the mirror again. What would Ty think? Would he like the change? Would he think I'm sexy?" Would he ask me out again? I was tempted to buy it. But what about my Grandmother? I could hear her firm voice in my ears. I could hear the straightening comb hit against the metal grill on the stove. The smell of pressed hair and scented grease filled the kitchen. I must have been 13 at the time. And, we were having one of our long Saturday talks.

"Virtue-- that's what I expect from you," Grandmah would say. " And that's what God wants, she parted my hair and pulled a warm comb through it.

Virtue? I thought, but I didn't open my mouth. I knew I was in the wrong so I sat quietly and listened.

"It's price is far higher than rubies," she quoted from the bible. She then glanced down at me to see if I was still listening.

I was.

"You're becoming a woman, Niara. And what you wear and how you act tell people a lot about you-- what kind of person you are."

I tried to nod my head, but the hot comb prevented me.

"There's nothing wrong with looking attractive. We all want that, but some clothes just give off a bad impression."

"I know," the words came out meekly.

"And sneaking out the house in hot-pants--

"They weren't--" I trailed off knowing it wasn't wise to correct Grandmah

She continued speaking, "Don't look right. It don't tell us a thing about you or your character. --showing off all you legs don't make you no more prettier than you already are, honey," she said knowing how it was to want the attention of a boy.

"I know you like Martin."

I swallowed hard. How did she know that? She seemed to know everything about me? I never imagined she'd find my cut-off jeans. I hid them so carefully. And, I only wore them when I thought it was safe.

"We all like people of the opposite sex, but you don't have to shed your clothes to show it. When I met your Grandpah, I didn't run out and buy a mini-shirt," she said gently.

Did they make them back then? I wondered.

As I listened to her talk, I knew my grandmother loved me. I heard what she said and I realized she was trying to protect me. From what? I had no idea, but I decided to accept the things she said.

"When a boy looks at you, Niara Saunders, I want him to see a young woman of quality. An intelligent woman who knows her value goes far beyond tight clothes, and a pretty face-- you hear me?"

"Yes Grandmah," I said.

"You're too precious for anything less," she smiled...

Kelli's voice interrupted my thoughts, "Are you going to stand there all day?"

"No," I said walking back to the dressing room. I took off the the jeans, halter top and shoes. I dressed quickly and gathered up all the things I wanted. But, I left the halter top hanging on the back of the door. My Grandmother's voice was still in my ears.

CHAPTER FOURTEEN

He pushed the rewind button again and waited. The tape back tracked until he stopped it. His fingers pushed play. Ominous words entered the environment of the car. They were the words of a rap song; but more significantly they were the words that reflected the history of the listener. The rap played like this:

"Old men, young boyz, drunks too
Gettin' all your booty after that they're through
Runnin' out your front door
Treatin' you like a whore
Why don't you stop them
Instead of askin' for more
One of these days I'm gonna bust them
One.
Two.
Three.
I might even bust you for lettin' me see
All my friends sayin', 'Your Mama's a whore'
Laughin', tauntin', busin', on me
'til I can't take it no more..."

The young man in the car hadn't seen his mother in nine

years. He left her back in New York with his brothers and sisters. He couldn't stay there anymore-- watching all the men in the neighborhood use his mother like a trash can. He had to get away.

He wondered what his brothers were doing now. He knew they wouldn't be in school, none of his family had graduated from high school. They were probably out running the street just as he had done. Doing anything to get away from home-- and his mother. He hoped his sisters weren't pregnant, but he knew better. What else did they have going for them?

These thoughts drifted away from him and he came back to the girl named Niara. Why was he even bothering with her he asked himself again? She wasn't his type. She was fine, but he could tell she was a kid. She was nothing like Nesha, his present ex, or Kimberly, or Tabatha, or Monique.

They were all out there when he met them. They all had kids by other brothers and were down with sex and everything. They wanted his money and he got what he wanted.

But, Niara didn't seem like that. He thought she had been in the beginning, but after talking to her he found out she wasn't. She was sixteen. She didn't have any kids. She tried to act like she was real tough, but he knew she wasn't. Sometimes she frightened him when she acted a little too shy. He wasn't use to girls turning red when he kissed them or looking down at the floor all of the time. He knew she was a virgin and that's when he started thinking maybe he should move on and leave her alone. He didn't want to hurt her. He didn't want to be her first lover. He was too old for that stuff.

Turning onto the avenue, he tucked his doubts to the back of his mind and drove the three blocks to Turner's mini-market.

131

CHAPTER FIFTEEN

"He's here," Kelli said rushing over to me from the other side of the cash register.

"I know," I said getting nervous. My mouth was extremely dry. I wanted to go out with him, but now that it was happening; I was too scared to do anything but look at his white car parked in front of the store.

"Go ahead. I can finish up here," she said nudging me to leave.

"I'm going."

"Is he really going to take you to see a play?" Kelli asked.

"I told you he was."

"I just don't get it. He ain't the type."

"He asked me what I wanted to do--"

"And you told him a play?"

"What's wrong with that?"

"You could've gotten him to take you anywhere. You could've gone to A C, to the casinos or up to New York. You could have been jamming all weekend long."

"You must be dreaming. First of all, Cathleen isn't going to let me go to a club-- in New York-- with him. And second, that's not what I want."

"No you'd prefer to sit in some dark theater watching some play."

"Don't make it sound so bad. You do the same thing when you go to the movies."

"There's a difference. People like movies. Don't nobody go to see plays," she said. "You'll be the only ones there."

"I don't care. I like plays. And he agreed to take me."

I grabbed my leather bag. I reached inside it and took out a thin plastic vial of muslim oil. Uncapping it, I emptied some of the slow moving liquid onto my skin.

"Is that all you got in mind?" she asked eyeing my actions suspiciously.

"Yes it is, but it doesn't hurt to smell good."

"What does that mean?"

"It means I might get kissed today," I said puckering up my lips and throwing her a kiss.

"Keep talking like that and I'm gonna have to call your mother and tell her about her daughter."

"Go ahead and try. She's at work," I said confidently.

"Girl you better be careful," she said seriously. "Don't let him move too fast. Make him take it slow."

"Take your own advise. I'm not the one spending all my time with Bill," I teased.

"Mind your business," she said pushing me toward the door. She was whispering in my ear now, "Don't let him touch you on the first date. He can kiss you but that's it. No grinding. Okay."

"I wasn't going to. But I can take care of myself."

"I don't know about that," said Kelli. "This is your first date. It's my responsibility to make sure your know how to act."

"Thank you mother," I said.

As I said goodbye to Kelli, I opened the door and stepped onto the sidewalk. The blaring words to a rap song immediately hit my ears. They were coming from the car parked at the curb...

"No mask on my face
Don't know my place, but
I'm invisible
Unless I'm gettin' physical
Buffin' floors
Limited doors
No cash in the bank
Can't afford to think, but
I'm invisible
Unless I'm gettin' physical
A nation razed
Lost in a white maze
Born, torn, scorned, but
I'm invisible
Unless I'm getting physical
Languishing in professional poverty
Brother man don't even bother me
'cause we're invisible
unless we're gettin' physical..."

I got into his car and we drove off.

CHAPTER SIXTEEN

'TAKING BACK THE NEIGHBORHOOD', opened to an audience of seven black people; an elderly man, three middle aged women, a parent of an actor who applauded too much, and Ty and me.

The faces of the seven people were obscured by the whiteness of the stage lights, but if the performers could have seen the faces they would have witnessed signs of expectation and excitement.

Two black men stood on center stage facing us. One was speaking, the other listening...

"We are doomed! Doomed to remain dumb black niggers if we keep on thinking like you. Do you really believe we are taking back our neighborhood? These drug dealers are our kids. They are our neighborhood," said Mark.

"Don't matter man. We gotta do something. Things are getting too outta hand."

"So we are supposed to collectively reject our kids? You want me to start a war against my own children instead of trying in some way to help them? Is that what you are asking me to do, John?"

"Look it's too late for all the sentimental stuff. I'm not saying we kill them off, but I think we need to let them know we aren't going to tolerate this mess anymore. If they want to sell drugs or shoot up a block, they are going to have to take the consequences that come with it."

"And how are you going to get that idea across?" inquired Mark.

"If we gotta knock some heads around, that's what we gotta do."

"No John. I don't want to be apart of that. Violence against these kids is not my answer."

"So what should we do? Stand by and let them destroy where we live? I can't accept that."

"No, we should not accept that. But maybe we are starting things too late. Maybe we should have been a father to some of these boys before they got to this point. Maybe some of this stuff is our fault."

"Blame yourself man. That's not my responsibility. I got my own kids to raise."

"You can say that John, but either way you still got to deal with the problem. But if you do it when they are young, they will listen to you. Right now they couldn't give a damn what you say. Being black and male is one hell of a combination. And when you don't got no man around to tell you what's what, it can be even worse."

"Being black is not what's on their mind, " said John. "They are too busy plotting who to stick up next..."

I could hear Ty moving around in his seat. We had been sitting close together until the play started. I thought we were going to hold hands and hopefully he would kiss me. He hadn't done it yet unless you counted the one in the drug store and that wasn't a real kiss. But he was too engrossed in the play to even think about kissing me.

When the play started, he immediately sat up with interest.

He couldn't take his eyes off the two men on stage. But as he watched, he also became angry. He spoke out loudly if he didn't agree with something said.

Ty startled me when he said, "What's he talking about? Robbing people is not the only thing on our mind. He needs to shut up 'cause he don't know what he's talking about."

Ty's outburst made me anxious and my attention was divided between him and the play for the entire two hours...

As we were leaving the theater, I asked, "Did you like it?"

"It was all right, but if somebody like John stepped to me, I'd have to hurt him. I ain't standing still and letting nobody beat on me. Can't believe he thinks the death penalty is going to help the black race-- all that means is that whites will be killing more of us off."

"I don't know about that," I said. "Crime affects so many people. Not just blacks."

"You say that because you don't have friends in jail. If you did, you'd know there are more niggers in the pen than you could count in a life time."

"I guess so. I hadn't thought about it."

"You don't need to guess Niara . I'm telling you so. I got friends on death row who I know don't belong there-- I'm not saying that's the case for all of them, but it lets me know there is a problem with the system."

"So what should we do?" I asked. "How do you stop all the drugs and killings?"

"Do like Mark said. Be a daddy to these boys before they get too grown. I would've listened to somebody like him if he'd been there when I was little."

"Your father wasn't around?"

"Don't know. If he was, nobody bothered to point him out to me."

"I didn't have a father either," I said.

"Looks like we got something in common after all."

"Why do you say that?"

"I thought you were this perfect little girl who came from this perfect little world."

"Not hardly," I said.

We walked to the car and continued to discuss the play. I told him how surprised I was about the ending; John had changed his mind and agreed with Mark that the answer was not to fight against the young black boys in the neighborhood-- that would just divide them further. Instead, both men decided to be surrogate fathers to all the children on their block. They began a program trying to encourage all concerned black men to do the same. Ty also thought the ending was good. Although, he still didn't like John too much.

As I got back into Ty's car, I realized that I really liked him. He was nothing like any boy I had met before. He was tough and street minded, but I was really starting to like him. And, I wanted him to kiss me-- not some butterfly kiss that you couldn't feel and wasn't sure even happened, but a real one. I knew it was coming, but when? The anticipation knotted my stomach up into a tight ball. When was he going to do it? In the car? At the corner of my block where he agreed to drop me off? When? When? When?

I thought about this all the way home, but it never happened.

CHAPTER SEVENTEEN

"Some boy called here for you-- said his name was Ty. Who is he?" Cathleen asked not allowing me time to get into the front door. I was returning home after spending the day at Kelli's house.

How long had she been waiting at the door for me? I didn't want to answer her. I didn't want to hear any warnings about boys and being too young to date.

"He's a friend."

"Where did you meet him?"

"Why?"

"I'm curious. How long have you been seeing him?"

"Who said I was seeing him?"

"I know you are Niara. How long?"

"About a month."

"Are you going with him?"

"What do you mean? Am I sleeping with him?"

"Are you his girlfriend, Niara?"

"And if I am? Are you going to tell me I can't? Why so many questions?"

"I could tell you who to be friends with, but that doesn't mean you'll listen to me," said Cathleen.

"Stop worrying. He's a nice boy."

"Are you going to let me meet him?"

"Why do you want to do that?"

"I'd like to know who your friends are."

139

"I'll see."

"I'm serious Niara. Getting involved with a boy is an important decision. I don't--"

"Oh boy. Here it comes. Please don't start telling me about all the mistakes you made with Dad, because I don't want to hear them. I'm not you and I'm not going to let some boy get me preg--" I stopped abruptly. I didn't mean to say that.

"I wasn't going to say anything like that. I just want you to pick your friend carefully."

"I told you he is a nice boy."

"How old is he?" she persisted. "He didn't sound like a boy to me."

"Stop questioning me."

"How old Niara?"

"I don't know."

"Niara!"

"I said I don't know."

"Niara please don't rush into anything."

"I'm not going to. I know what I'm doing."

"Things can happen before you know what's going on-- accidents can happen."

"I'm not thinking about having sex, but you are a little to late for the sex talk. I already know about condoms and AIDS," I said.

"How old is he?" Cathleen wasn't about to be distracted.

"He's twenty-three," I admitted reluctantly.

"Twenty-three! Oh my god. And he's calling here for you? He's no boy. He's a man. What does he want with a little girl like you?"

"I'm not a little girl," I corrected.

"Oh no? Since when? At sixteen that's all you are."

"I don't have to listen to this. We are just friends. I don't know what you are so upset about-- I shouldn't have told you anything about him."

"But Niara, he's going to eventually want more than your friendship."

"You don't know what you're talking about. We are just friends."

"Don't kid yourself."

"And if he does want more?" I asked. "So what. I can take care of myself. I know how to say no."

"I don't want him calling here," said Cathleen. "He's too old."

"And if I tell him not to call here what is that going to mean? I'll still see him if that's what I want. And that is what I want."

"No Niara. I won't let you do that."

"How are you going to stop me?" I said walking pass her and up the stairs to use the telephone in her room. I wasn't trying to be disrespectful to Cathleen. She didn't know Ty, he wasn't a dog. We didn't talk about sex. We kissed and held hands.

I dialed his number and made arrangements for him to pick me up after Cathleen went to work.

CHAPTER EIGHTEEN

HIT N RUN THAT'S HOW I GIT IT
NO NEED ME PRETENDIN'
I AIN'T DOWN WIT IT!
HIT IT HARD
RUN MY GAME FAST
OUT THE DOOR
'CAUSE IT AIN'T GONNA LAST
HIT N RUN THAT'S THE PURE HIGH
COSTS ME NOTHING, BUT A BIT OF MY TIME
HER BODY'S MINE
SHE DOES WHAT I SAY
'CAUSE SHE'S STUPID
AND I LIKE HER THAT WAY
HIT N RUN THAT'S HOW I GIT IT
NO NEED ME PERPETRATIN'
I AIN'T DOWN WIT IT!
TOO MANY FOXY BROWNS
LOOKIN FOR LOVE
WILLIN TO OBEYIN' MY EVERY WORD... the young
black man mouthed the words silently as he drove down the
crowded, narrow street for the third time--in front of him was a
Capri, and behind him was a Prelude, but he wasn't intimidated
'cause he had the Lexus. And, he knew all eyes were upon him.
He leaned back allowing the leather to caress his body. He wore a

tee-shirt and an intricately designed gold necklace. His eyes were concealed by expensive sunglasses which did not hinder his search for something sweet, young and naive. South Street was packed. Before his eyes, marched a parade of girls-- most of them were young, but too silly to consider hittin'. They lacked the elegance he required. They were cute, but not his type.

He drove on.

Then he spotted her. He watched her round butt move seductively in a pair of denim shorts. A smile touched his lips. He liked big legs, and hers were definitely that. They were well formed and muscular. His eyes slid up her back to rest on straight shoulders and a prominently raised head. Tiny braids adorned her head. He hoped the front looked as good.

Kevin casually glanced at her as his car inched by. The traffic was heavy. This gave him time to decide if she was worth it or not. Her face was pretty, but what really got him was her body. Her breast bounced gently as she sashayed down the street. Her flat stomach revealed itself each time she laughed at whatever her girlfriend was saying...

"What's your name shortie?" his voice was melodic.

"Kelli," she said turning her head to the rhythm in his voice.

"What chu doing out here on a Friday night?"

"Shopping, Why you want to know?"

"Maybe I'd like to buy you something."

"But you don't know me--" she began flirtatiously.

The girl at her side became impatient, "Come on Kelli. I got to get home. It's late."

"Wait a minute Niara," she whispered.

"No," I said softly.

"Let's see what he wants," Kelli insisted.

"I know what he wants. And so do you," I declared.

Kelli gave me a hard look, "And what's that?"

"Never mind," I said backing off. I didn't feel like arguing with Kelli today about some boy.

"What do you want to buy me?" she flirted back.

"I don't know--" he paused. "What do you want?" he asked creeping down the street with the two girls trying to keep up. Kelli had her hand in Niara's and wouldn't let go.

Kelli let out a giggle. She was impressed with her charms. Never before had she been approached by a guy in a car like this. She couldn't believe her luck. Her slanted eyes gleamed with joy. He wanted to talk to her, Kelli.

" I'm hungry. What about you?" she asked.

"You like seafood?" he smiled liking the way things were going. "Get in," he said unlocking the passenger's door. He casually eyed the girl next to Kelli. She was attractive too, but a little too skinny for his taste. But her eyes, they made him do a double-take. Once she filled out a bit, she'd be something else. Then he thought, if they both were down with it-- he'd hit them both a couple of times before the night was out. He was young, why not?

"I don't think we should do this?" I said hesitantly.

"Come on Niara. Stop playing games."

"I'm serious," I said pulling her away from the car. "I'm not getting in there."

"Why not?" she stared at me.

"We don't know him," I said softly. I didn't want to embarrass her by getting loud.

"So what? You didn't know Ty but you got in his car."

"That's different," I said.

"How?"

"Ahhh-- you knew him," I said realizing that was not a good explanation either.

"Don't give me that," she said trying to shake my hand free. "If you don't want to go that's fine, but I am."

I stood still. I didn't know what to do. I could see she meant it, but I didn't trust him.

"Kelli. I'm your friend. I'd stand by you no matter what? But this is dangerous. You get in that car and he can take you anywhere-- do anything to you."

"I'm not that kind of brother," said Kevin feigning hurt feelings.

" If you feel that way then, get in the car with me?" she begged. She wasn't about to blow this because of Niara. He had money. And he was willing to spend it on her. That's more than most of these sorry brothers around here wanted to do.

"No," I said getting desperate.

"Then see you later," she said stepping off the curb. She walked quickly around the front of the car, and was about to grab the door's handle.

I couldn't let her do it. I knew I looked stupid, but so what? Maybe next week she'd forgive me. I didn't care.

I ran around the car and snatched her hand way from the door. I wasn't strong, but I threw my arms around her body and tried to pick her up.

"Get off of me Niara!" she yelled not thinking this was funny. "What are you doing?"

"Friends don't let friends do stupid things," I whispered in her ear.

"Girl you're crazy!" she said struggling to get free. "I should have known something was wrong with you when I found you sitting in that park. Now let go of me."

"No," I said.

The guy in the car beeped his horn at us, "I'll catch y'all later," he said ready to move on. They were becoming too much of an effort. And with that, the Lexus took off.

Kelli couldn't believe her eyes. "You made him leave me!" she yelled finally shaking me free. "I don't believe this. He was interested in me! And you got jealous? Niara I hate you," she said stepping away from the moving traffic.

"It's not like that," I tried to explain.

"Yes it is," she said.

"Kelli I--"

"Get away from me," the other girl threatened. "Before I hurt you. I mean it Niara Saunders. You ain't my friend," she said stepping back onto the pavement. "I'm going home. Alone!"

I knew what that meant. So I hung back and watched her walk down the street. Had I done the wrong thing? Did this guy really like her? Did I blow it?

I felt guilty, but in my heart I knew I was right.

CHAPTER NINETEEN

I TRAILED BEHIND HER until I couldn't take it anymore. This was stupid. She was mad at me because I wouldn't let her get into a car with a stranger? She was going to throw our friendship away-- just like that? Over a boy?

I was getting angrier and angrier as I thought about it.

"You know you're wrong!" I yelled out to her.

She ignored me.

"We're supposed to be friends," I said deciding to catch up with her. Everybody didn't have to know our business.

"Kelli? Aren't you going to say something.

She just looked at me and rolled her eyes.

"I wasn't acting jealous. Honest. I just didn't want anything bad to happen to you. You're my best friend."

"You did not have to do that to me."

"But you weren't listening--"

"I don't have to. I can make up my own mind."

"I know you can, but--"

"Ain't no buts. I decide what I want to do-- understand?"

"No," I said standing my ground. "If we're together, then we both decide what we are going to do. And if you want to do something crazy, I'm not going to be quiet-- understand?" I said softening the last part of my statement.

Kelli looked at me and tried to roll her eyes again.

"And don't be cutting your eyes at me," I said shoving her.

"Cutting?" Kelli raised an eyebrow. "Who have you been

listening to?"

"My Grandmah. But it doesn't matter" I smiled. "You get the point. Don't be treating my like some enemy."

"All right," she said.

"Friends?" I asked.

"Always," she smiled. "You want to get some ice cream from McDonalds? My treat."

"Yeah," I said.

We walked down the street best friends again.

CHAPTER TWENTY

You are the genesis of my dream
in a world filled with radiant scenes
a kiss, a touch, a lullaby for two
a gentle embrace
I love you
My heart pounds
at a single glance
Your eyes dazzle me at every chance
You are the epic of my world— Najee Brown
controlled the basketball with his right hand as he walked down
the street. Its bthump, bthump, bthump was in synch with the
words forming in his head. His long, lean fingers stroked the
surface of the ball as he maneuvered it across a wide city street.
His strides were graceful. His steps agile and precise. He knew
the game and was second to few. His dark mahogany face
glistened with a light sweat as he quickened his pace with the rock.

His thoughts left the unfinished poem. He refused to get
frustrated by its incompleteness. He knew after years of writing
that eventually the words would come. He couldn't rush them.

Instead, his mind went to Kelli.

He hated crushes; he couldn't be bothered with them. He
had too much stuff planned for his future. He was going to be a
commercial pilot. Go to college. Get out of this city. And, do

something for a change. He didn't want to be trapped-- not like his father.

ANTHONY BROWN had seven boys and he didn't take care of any of them. They were wards of his mother. And she alone supported them. The only help she got was from the people in the community who gave her clothes, and food when times got hard. The neighborhood was kind; it adopted the seven children and was always on the watch for them. If the children needed discipline and their mother wasn't around, an elderly person would offer words of correction or a gentle phrase if they needed it.

Najee had no complaints. He love the people in West Philadelphia. They helped to raise him. And they expected a lot from him. His mother had it hard, and he didn't want to recreate that same situation for a girl. Yes his father married his mother, but so what. He also left her. He was in jail now. Locked up for 20 years. Najee stopped waiting for him a long time ago. By the time Anthony got out, Najee wouldn't need a father.

What was he going to do about Kelli?

He had hopes and now one girl was messing things up for him. She had walked into his world and caused chaos. He could almost smile if it wasn't so serious. He was leaving for college in a month. Najee had managed to avoid girls-- all girls, but Kelli. She had forced her way into his world. And now he didn't want to lose her.

He remember their first meeting as he dribbled the ball on the sidewalk near the playground. He allowed a smile to grace his lips. Was he in love? Hell no! But he did like her a lot.

He was on his way to see her.

His smile broaden, accentuating high cheekbones and an amazing pair of eyes. Every day at this time, Kelli and he would play a game of one on one. Of course, she never beat him, but that didn't mean she wasn't good. He was forever encouraging her to try out at school. He knew she'd get picked. She was awesome.

Najee arrived at the court, but didn't see Kelli. He checked out the swings--that was her favorite spot. She wasn't there. He caught the ball to his chest and walked to the nearest bench. He dropped down onto its wooden surface. He threw his head back and closed his eyes. He'd give her fifteen minutes. His face was still damp and the slight breeze felt good to him.

"You'll lose this time," a soft voice whispered in his ear.

Najee didn't open his eyes. He simply smiled and enjoyed her scent. He liked tangerine. He could smell the fragrance in her hair. Everything about Kelli was exciting.

"I guess you've been practicing."

"I have."

"And now you think you're good?" he said opening his eyes for the first time.

"Don't have to think. I know," she corrected snatching up the ball from its position beside him on the bench. "Come on."

"Wait," he said.

"Why?

"I want to talk."

"About?"

"Us," he said.

Kelli made her way back to the bench; she sat the ball down, "What about us?"

"I'm leaving for Lincoln in three weeks."

"I know," she said softly.

"And I won't be back until Christmas. But I like you Kelli. And I want our friendship to continue."

"Me too," she said coyly.

"Can you and your mom come to my house for dinner?" he asked out of nowhere."

"Huh?"

"This Sunday. At 3 o'clock."

"I guess so, but why? You ain't gonna ask me to marry you?" she teased.

He smiled, "Why'd I want to do that?"

"Don't ask me. You're the one making all the plans."

"I just think our families should meet-- get to know each other. Isn't your mother curious about me?"

"No."

"Why not?" he questioned.

" 'cause I didn't tell her about you. She's too busy doing other things."

"Oh," he paused. "Do you think she'll come?"

"Yeah. Does your mother know about me?"

"Almost as much as I do," he said glancing down at her.

"Really?"

"Really. And she's anxious to meet you. I told her you were a nice girl. And that I liked you a lot."

"You do?"

"Stop pretending Kelli. You know I do."

"You better," she said leaning over to give him a quick kiss. Then she jumped up and grabbed the ball. "Race you to the court," before he could respond, Kelli was running down the

152

basketball court.

She could hear him in the distance, "Cheater!"

CHAPTER TWENTY ONE

"It's hard to believe you are only sixteen-- especially looking like that."

"Well I am," I said shyly.

"You definitely don't look like it."

I took a big bite of my chicken cheese-steak hoagie and looked out of the window. I liked it when Ty talked about the way I looked. It made me feel special. I felt like he really meant it. Whenever he talked this way, I always ended up saying something stupid. And this time was no exception.

"Damn this hoagie is delicious."

Damn? When did I start using that word. I was beginning to sound like Kelli. The word sounded strange coming from my lips.

Could Ty tell I was uneasy. Did my behavior show it? He had parked his car on a narrow pathway obscured by large trees. We were totally alone. The only sound I heard besides us was a car going by every once in a while.

Ty unwrapped his hoagie completely and opened his beer before he began to eat. He was nothing like me when it came to eating. He took his time getting his food ready. He was not in a rush to gulp it down, like I was.

He took a bite of his fish hoagie before he commented, "You don't look anything like your mother-- who do you take after?"

"I don't know," I shrugged. "Maybe one of my dead

154

owners," I joked a little off key.

Ty had finally met my mother after weeks and weeks of her pressuring me. I don't know why I agreed to it, she still didn't trust him. She kept begging me to talk to boys my own age. Why didn't she understand? I didn't like anybody, but Ty.

"We probably all look like them," he said. "Your mother doesn't have eyes like yours. You got intense, sexy eyes."

I smiled.

I watched him eat. I watched him finish his hoagie and recap the bottle of beer he had just emptied.

"Ty," I started. "Why don't you take me out anymore? We used to do a lot of things-- go places together," I said picking at my onion rings.

"You don't like the way I treat you, Niara?"

"I didn't say that," I stopped speaking and then began again. "I'm supposed to be your girlfriend and we don't do anything or go anywhere. Not even to the movies."

"What are you trying to tell me?"

"I don't like this. We don't see each other a lot-- and when we do, it's always in your car. I want to do things."

"I can't spend all my time with you Niara."

"I know."

"I'm a busy man. I don't have time to take you to all the places I did before. I'm working for different people now. Don't you understand that?"

"I understand. I just wanted to see you more. I'm tired of only seeing you at night. I don't like sneaking out the house after Cathleen goes to work. Why can't I see you during the day?"

"In the future baby, when I don't need to work so much."

I said nothing. Instead, I stuffed my trash into a paper bag and wiped my mouth with a napkin.

"Are you finished with the complaints?" he asked.

"I wasn't complaining. I miss seeing you," I said truthfully.

"Then get over here next to me," he said. He looked good with the herring bone draped across his neck. Ty definitely knew how to dress. He always wore expensive track suits and sneakers. His clothes always smelled brand new, like this was the first time he'd put them on. I never planned on falling for someone like him. But, I liked his black smooth skin, his warm brown eyes, and his juicy brown lips that sometimes revealed white teeth.

I didn't move. I instead popped a piece of gum into my mouth to kill the onion taste.

"What's wrong?" he asked noticing I didn't react to his request.

"I don't want to do that right now."

"What?"

"Kissing. Can't we talk for a change?"

"Go ahead. Talk," he said throwing up his hands.

"I meant instead of doing all that touching."

"Say what's on your mind."

I was quiet. One minute passed. Two minutes. Three...

"Look Niara," he said climbing over the divider separating the passenger seat from the driver. He pulled me to him. I didn't resist.

"I like you a lot," he said. "I know you ain't used to all this. I'm trying to be patient, but don't expect me to be something I'm not."

"I wasn't," I said defensively.

He began to rub my knee. It was slow and persuasive. He was trying to coax me into relaxing. I tried to relax.

"Do you like this?"

"I guess so," I said flatly. I should have been honest and said no. How was he going to know I hated it if I didn't tell him.

"What about this?" he asked running his fingertips down the sides of my legs and back up again to the warmth of my inner legs.

But instead I said, "It's okay."

"I want you to feel good, relax," he said softly.

"I'm trying."

His hands gradually crept from under the hem of my shorts and they moved very slowly, very precisely up the front of my shirt. I began to feel and uneasiness erupt inside my stomach. He was inching toward my breast. I caught his hand with mine.

"Don't do that."

"Why not?" he asked.

"I don't want you to touch me there."

"I promise you'll like it," he whispered in my hair.

"No."

He didn't put up an argument. He simply resumed rubbing my legs and I tried to relax. We sat like that for a long time. I tried rubbing his leg-- his thigh to be specific. It felt firm and strong, but I was too uneasy to like it. I didn't dare move my hands any further. My rubbing was fixed to one small area on his leg. I was afraid to move from that spot. My inexperienced hands were paralyzed. My eyes were glued to my hands. I was afraid to look at him. I was almost to afraid to breathe.

"Do you know what I want Niara?"

"What?" I asked hesitantly.

"To have sex with you," he said simply.

"No," I whispered. I wasn't even sure if he heard me.

He began playing in my hair-- racking his fingernails against my scalp, almost combing my hair. I could feel him undoing my hair. He threw my hair piece onto the dashboard.

"Your hair feels like silk. All of you feels like silk baby."

"I can't."

"Why not?" he continued to rub my leg. "You're my girl aren't you?"

"Yes."

"And I know you like me."

"I do."

"And I know you trust me," he continued to speak.

"I do."

"So why not have sex with me?"

"Because I'm not ready for it. I can't deal with the responsibilities of it."

"What responsibilities? All you have to do is enjoy it."

"I can't."

"I promise you won't get pregnant."

"I want to-- to wait."

"Wait for what? Until you get married?" he said cynically.

"Yes."

"Well baby you're going to be waiting a long, long time. And if you think I'm waiting that long, you're crazy," he said jokingly.

"Don't laugh at me! I didn't ask you to wait. You can do

whatever you want. I don't care."

"Don't say things you don't mean Niara. I may take you up on it."

"Then don't make fun of me."

"All right, all right. There's nothing wrong with the idea of waiting, but be realistic. Not having sex until you're twenty-whatever is crazy. You won't last."

"I am being realistic."

"Niara you're dreaming. Nobody waits for marriage anymore."

"I don't care. I am waiting."

"So what am I supposed to do? And what was all that about?" he asked looking down at my hand resting on his leg. I snatched it away.

"I-- was trying to make you happy."

"And now that I'm feeling good, what are you going to do about it?"

"Nothing," I mumbled.

"Are you teasing me Niara?"

"You know I'm not."

"Are you sure?" he demanded.

"Yes. I wouldn't do that."

"I don't know. Lately I'm not too sure about anything."

"I'm sorry Ty," I said because I knew I had disappointed him.

"I can't live like this Niara. I'm telling you now. I got you saying no, no, no and then I got other girls including my ex throwing their stuff at me. You tell me what am I supposed to do? I like you, but this isn't going to work."

I was quiet. I looked down, because I didn't want him see the tears. My heart was gradually beginning to stop. I didn't want him to dump me. I didn't want him to tell me he was thinking about having sex with somebody else. I didn't like feeling jealous. How could you be jealous of girls you didn't know? I wasn't sure how, but that's what I was feeling.

Why couldn't he wait? Was that really too much to ask?

"Are you having sex with them?" I asked feeling like someone had stuck a sock down my throat. I felt like my heart was being ripped apart by thousands of long red fingernails.

"No," he said.

"But you want to?" I whispered. I still couldn't look at him. It hurt too much.

"I don't know." he said lifting my face and forcing me to look at him. "Would it matter if I did?"

"Yes," I said allowing him to see my tears.

"This just isn't going to work Niara. Somebody's going to get hurt."

"But why? If you like me, why can't you wait?"

"Because if I do that, we can only be friends? Do you know what that means?"

"No."

"That I'll be having sex with someone else-- is that what you want?" he asked.

"Why are you saying that?"

"Because it's true," he said releasing my face and getting back into the driver's seat. "Come on. I'm taking you home."

I didn't say a word. I sat back and let him drive me to the corner of my block.

CHAPTER TWENTY TWO

"Burn the Constitution! Burn it now!
'cause the black man's not equal
you show me how.
He's livin' in a racist world and there he'll die.
No bill of rights to protect him
'cause you know it's a lie.
Burn them papers.
Turn them yellow pages brown.
Then sell them ashes like they sold Mama Powell..."

The rap filled the car with its angry words. It's powerful message merged with the windows, doors, and walls of the car. The words were so forceful they spilled over the half open window and into the deaf streets where no one would bother to listen. The words were diluted by the busyness of the streets-- they disappeared and the street was oblivious to their anger.

He looked cute, I thought to myself as I walked up to his parked car. It had been weeks since the last time we had seen each other. Before he left, he told me he had to take care of some personal business in New York. I think one of his brothers had gotten into some trouble and needed his help.

I wanted to smile when I saw him, but I couldn't. My mouth wouldn't let me. My lips felt numb-- like I just came from the dentist. He was leaning on the car. I told him I'd be getting off at six, and now he was here waiting for me.

"I've missed you," he said walking up to me and kissing me slightly on the lips.

I stared at his mouth-- his lips. They were cool and soft. I liked the feel, the way they touched my own. I tried to smile again, but it got lost in the attempt. He gave me a big smile. The kind that would make ice cream melt.

"Get in," he said.

I couldn't move. I was very nervous and excited and hot, all at the same time. I tried to say something but my mouth filled with saliva. And my tongue got twisted into knots.

"Niara?" he looked at me with some concern. "What's wrong?"

"Nothing--" I tried to say more but my words became hoarse.

He reached out. Grabbing my hands, he pulled me to him. What was he going to do, I wondered? He bent his head down again and kissed me in the mouth, but this time as he did so he whispered against my lips, "I've been waiting for a long, long, long time to be alone with you. Come on girl," he said. "I got you something."

He held the door open for me and I got in. He slammed it shut. As he walked around the front of the car to get in the driver's seat, I started looking for my something. It wasn't on the front seat. It wasn't in the glove compartment. It wasn't on the floor. I looked in the back seat-- nothing. Where was it? I knew it wasn't at his house, because I'd never been there before. It had to be in the car.

"It's not here," I said disappointedly. "Is it in the trunk?"

"No."

"What is it?"

"You'll see later," he said.

"All right."

I wasn't thrilled about waiting, but I settled back against the leather seats. I took a deep breath and inhaled all the newness of his car. I always liked the smell of new things-- new shoes, new books, new clothes.

"Where are we going?" I asked.

"To Lee Avenue. I got to talk to somebody.

"Fine. I want to buy a pack of gum. I forgot to get some at Turner's"

I accepted his answer. I knew not to ask who. He had made it clear to me a long time ago not to ask him direct questions when he did not volunteer specific information.

"I'm not staying long. Don't hold me up."

"I won't."

He stopped the car. I hadn't been paying attention so I did not see Ty drive up to the curve. He turned the car off and took the keys from the ignition and got out.

I spotted a corner store and got out and headed for it. The building was very small, but had the same assortment of foods and canned goods you would find at a supermarket. The floor was a dry, muddy swirl made by too many people tracking in the morning's rain. Someone had placed a flattened cardboard box on the floor in an attempt to absorb some of the water. But, the box simply made the mess worse. An overpowering smell was in the air. It was raw fish lying on a small amount of ice-- too small of an amount to be considered safe for human consumption. Because of the pungent odor, it was seldom that a customer's nose was allowed to savor the smell of homemade cookies baked by the black woman behind the counter. If they were permitted, the cookies would offer a strong, delicious smell. But, there was no way that they could compete with the fish.

I looked around the store. A Korean owner was restocking dark red tomatoes in the produce section. He had on a dirty apron to match his dirty worn-down Nike sneakers. His appearance did not seem to bother him, but I wondered if his tomatoes were as dirty as he.

"Can I have a pack of watermelon gum and two chocolate chip cookies?"

She met my request with a pleasant response. She gave me a genuine smile. It was not one of those prepackaged smiles, like the ones most fast food restaurants used. I felt it was sincere.

"Thank you," I said before leaving the store.

Today was going to be a perfect day for me. It had already begun that way. For the first time in months, I was happy. I had my mother. And, I had Ty. What could be better? This morning Cathleen and I went shopping. We stopped at the Reading Terminal to buy peppered cheese and somehow we ended up taste testing imported cheeses, strange looking salads, and delicious smelling lunch meats. We got one pound of 'Neptune salad', and a half a pound of turkey salad with grapes and some kind of sweet salad dressing. We sample our way from the deli to the bakery section of the terminal which was only two counters over. Cathleen ended up buying much more than she had planned. I convinced her to buy me chocolate walnut cookies; she also bought a few other things before we left the terminal. We ate the cookies together as we window shopped. She was reaching into my bag so frequently that I had to remind her whose cookies they were. And then she reminded me that she had paid for them. Cathleen bought us matching tee-shirts and jeans and sneakers. I don't usually wear sneakers, but it seemed like everything in my life was changing. Why fight it? My life was perfect. And Ty made it even better.

I walked back towards the car. I stopped when I noticed two girls bending over and looking inside of it.

One girl was looking through the passenger's window. I heard her say, "Yeah this is Tyress's car. I told you it was. He ain't in no New York."

The other girl said nothing. She looked up and down the street. I guess she was searching for Ty. I stood rooted to my spot. I wasn't sure what to do. I did not know either girl and I didn't want to get in the middle of anything.

"Maybe he's back early," said Nesha. She was tall, dark and very pretty. She had on blue jeans and they showed off her too big butt and wide hips. It wasn't evident if her breast were as big as the rest of her. A red shirt hid this fact. Her ears looked like they were going to drop off because of the metal earrings tugging persistently at them.

"I don't think he got back early. I think he's been lying to you-- I saw a girl get out of this car," remarked Tobby.

"Maybe you're wrong."

"No I'm not. This was the car," she insisted.

"Then what did she look like?"

"A light skinned chick. I saw her while you was in the store buying your cigarettes."

"Tyress better not be cheating on me. I ain't taking it this time."

"Get ready to be one upset sister."

"I'm not gonna be calm about it this time. I'll kick his butt and any girl I catch him with. I swear I will," said Nesha.

"You better get ready, because here he comes," warned Tobby.

"Where?"

"Across the street," she pointed.

Before Tobby could say more, Nesha was rushing across the street toward him. It was a half run half walk. She was hot and her body moved like it.

"Who is she Tyress?" demanded Nesha.

"Huh? What are you talking about?"

"You know. I'm talking about the girl who was in your car. Who is she?"

"Nesha stop talking crazy. What girl? I ain't with nobody."

"You're lying. Tobby saw her get out of your car."

"She was wrong. I came here by myself. And don't be confronting me like this. I'll do what I want to. Now back off me."

"Look," Nesha began, stumbling over her words in an effort to apologize. "If I was wrong, I'm sorry--"

She would have said more, but Tobby's shouting halted her. Nesha was directed to look across the street at me. I immediately became paralyzed.

"You lying dog! I'm gonna kick her white butt," she said turning away from Ty and running across the street to me. She was too angry to pay attention to the cars or the trolley traveling the street. My frozen state disappeared quickly as I realized the danger I was in. I tried to get out of her way.

"Where are you going girl?" she demanded. "If you want my man, why don't you talk to me about it? I know you ain't scared of me," she said catching up to me. "You sure wasn't when you was messing with Tyress."

Nesha was breathing hard. Her heavy panting filled my ears. The smell of her cologne and sweat made me nauseous. She grabbed me by the shoulders. My eyes barely had time to focus on the other girl's face before my eye felt the impact of something hard. I saw a white fiery light before my eye went sightless.

"Ohhh!" I screamed putting my hands up to defend myself, but the punches kept coming.

"I didn't know he had a girlfriend--"

"Yeah right-- like you really care if he did," she hollered pulling at my hair.

I felt sharp nails ripping at my scalp. I swore I could feel hot blood running from the pain in my head. My face was on fire; my other eye had scratches obscuring its vision. I struggled desperately to understand what was happening to me.

"Git that white girl!" yelled Tobby.

I heard my shirt ripping. My hair was all over my head as I swung wildly into the air praying my hands would come into contact with some part of the other girl's body. My attempts hardly succeeded at anything other than causing me to become tired.

"Ty! Ty! Ty!" I screamed hysterically.

"Don't be calling my man!" she said, hitting me in the face again. "He ain't gonna help you now."

167

"Stop it! Stop it!" I continued to scream until the punches quieted my efforts.

"Nesha get off her," I finally heard a male voice. "What the hell are you doing?" he attempted to separate us.

"Don't touch me!" ordered Nesha. "I'm not going to be nobody's fool-- let me loose."

"I said let her go," said Ty.

"You make me," she said punching at his face and chest. "I hate you-- you ain't nothing but a lying, cheating dog."

"You don't want to play rough with me Nesha," he warned.

"Kiss my butt!"

"What did I tell you about talking to me like that?" the anger in his face was mounting.

His black skin was glossy from physical exertion. His hair was damp, showing off soft waves.

His anger was displayed so swiftly that Nesha did not have time to register what was happening. She felt a tight, hard grip encircling her neck. Then five fingers palmed her face. The pressure of each fingertip was brutal. She felt his fingerprints embedding themselves into her soft skin. She became frightened for the first time as she felt him drag her face close to his.

He whispered in her ear as he increased the intensity of his hold, "I told you to stop."

"Yes," she murmured.

"That sounds better--"

From behind Ty, I heard Tobby say, "Leave her alone or I'll bust your head wide open."

"Come on Tobby if you think you can do that."

"You don't believe me?" she challenged.

"I know you won't."

Tobby threw a bottle at him. It hit him on the shoulder, but refused to break.

"You stupid--" he said trying to get to her. He did not release his hold on Nesha. He carried her forward with him.

"Tyress--" she began crying. "Please--"

"I'm not letting you go yet. If you caused me any problems with Niara, I'm going to kick your butt."

"But you can't do that--" she whimpered. "Not to me. I'm your girl-- I thought you really cared about me."

"Girl don't you start that. I told you exactly how I was. Don't go pretending we had more than we did," he said releasing her. She staggered backward, but did not fall. He didn't care if she did or didn't. He was tired of her.

Ty turned to me cowering in a bent position on the curb of the street. He walked over to me and stooped down.

"Niara? Are you all right?"

No answer came from my lips.

"You're not going to push me aside just like that!" said Nesha interrupting his next words. "Don't nobody do me like that! You show me some respect!"

With those words, Nesha searched the sidewalk and street for a weapon. Any weapon. Seeing another forty ounce beer bottle, she grasped it by the neck and turned it upside down. She ignored the stale beer spilling onto the side of her hand. Rushing up to him, she hit him across his outstretched forearm. It broke and glass and alcohol sprayed his clothes.

"Don't be trying to treat me like some slut," she said running down an alley way. She thought he was chasing her, but he wasn't. Tobby joined her.

"Niara," he said looking down at the top of my head. "Look at me."

I obeyed him as best I could, "I-- can't see out of my eye."

"Let me see," he said staring into my face. "You're going to have a black eye-- your left one is almost closed now."

"What about the other one?"

"It looks black too. Come on baby let's get out of here," he said helping me up from the curb.

I let him help me. But then, I pulled away, "No! I can do it myself."

"Don't get like that Niara. You need my help."

"Who was she?" This was all I wanted to know.

"Some crazy girl I know."

"But-- she said you were her-- man?"

"Don't worry about that now. I need to get you to the car."

"She said I was screwing her man. Are you her boyfriend?"

"Don't start asking me questions right now. Let's go."

"I'm not going anywhere with you. I just got beat up-- and I want to know why."

"I told you, she's crazy."

"I don't believe you."

"Get in the car," he said opening the passenger's door.

I did.

Ty got in but, he didn't get a chance to pull away from the curb, because he saw blue and white lights flashing behind him.

"Damn!" he exclaimed looking into his rearview mirror. He watched two officers get out of their car.

"Is this your car?" a white policeman asked leaning into the open window.

"What do you think?"

"Give me your license and registration papers."

"Why? What did I do?" asked Ty.

"Don't ask me questions. Do it."

"Here," he said giving up the papers. "It's all legal. You ain't got nothing on me."

"What about her?" asked the black female officer leaning into the passenger's window. "Is she legal too?"

"Yes she is. What's it to you?" he asked.

The woman looked at me, "What happened to you?"

I turned to Ty. He gave me a 'keep your mouth shut look' and I did just that.

"How did your face get like that?" she asked. "Are you the girl we got the call about?"

"I don't think so," I mumbled.

"You fit the description," she persisted.

"So do a lot of girls around here," said Ty. "It's not her."

The white officer then spoke, "How old are you?"

"She's old enough," he said.

"What kind of crack is that?" demanded the male officer.

"It means she's old enough to hang."

"Keep talking and I'll take you down to the round-house and let you hang there for a couple of hours."

'Hey sister, are you going to let him do that? Threaten me for no reason," he said smiling.

"I didn't hear a threat," she said smiling back at Ty.

"Did you do that to her?" asked the male officer.

"I'm not like that. I was about to give her a ride home."

171

"You look fifteen," said the black woman.

I said nothing.

"Sixteen?" she refused to give up.

I don't know why I nodded, but I did.

By this time, the white officer had walked away from the car. He had Ty's papers in his hand.

"Who beat you up?" she wanted to know.

Ty spoke for me, "She don't know."

"Was it those girls over there?" she asked pointing to somebody.

I didn't bother to look, "No."

"I'm not getting anywhere with you in that car. Get out," said the black officer.

"Why?" I asked.

"Because I want to get some answers from you and it's not going to happen if you are sitting next to him."

"Don't do it Niara."

"But she told me to--"

"You haven't done anything. You do not have to go with her."

"Get out Niara," she repeated.

"Don't do it. She ain't got nothing on either of us. She's just trying to intimidate you."

I moved to open the door. I didn't want to stay in the car with him. I hurt badly and just wanted to go home.

"I'm going."

"If you do that, don't expect to come back."

"Don't come back?" I was tired and feed up. "After what your girlfriend did to me, you won't have to worry about me coming back," I said.

"Shut up Niara."

"You need to shut your own mouth," said the black officer. "You got no business with somebody her age. She's a kid. What are you trying to do, turn her out?"

"Maybe I'll turn you out," he smiled.

She looked at him blankly, "And maybe I'll shoot your black butt."

Ty stopped grinning.

She continued, "That's what's wrong with this neighborhood-- people like you. I'm so tired of seeing your type manipulate little girls like her. Do you ever think about what it's like being used?"

"What are you talking about?" he asked.

"Of course you don't," she said harshly. "I was expecting to much from you. Get out of the car Niara."

I unlocked the car and stepped out into the black street. I felt nauscous. What was she going to do to me? I followed her away from the car.

"Are they the girls who did that to you?" she repeated. I began to think she was a recording.

"Not that question again. Does it matter now?"

"Yes it does."

"No they aren't the ones," I lied.

"Are you saying you don't know who jumped you?"

"No. I just want to forget the whole thing."

"I hate this stuff," she muttered. "Why are you with him."

"He's my boyfriend."

"What do you know about a boyfriend? You're a child--

and he's a damn man!"

"I'm sixteen," I defended.

"Are you screwing him?"

"Huh? That's none of your business."

"Everyday I see this stuff-- girls like you dealing with men like that. Doing any and everything they tell you to. And do you know who always gets hurt? Girls like you. By the time we get to you, it's usually too late."

I stared at her. Her words were giving me a chilling feeling.

"Most of the girls are turned completely out. They are either screwing all his friends because he told them too or they are hooked on something-- don't become another one of those girls."

"But Ty's not like that."

"Yes I know. None of them are ever like that until it happens."

"But he's not."

"How do you know?" she asked.

"Because he likes me," I said lamely.

"No honey. Don't be fooled. He likes the way you look-- how good you make him look. You are no different to him than any other pretty girl. You are simply fitting the profile."

"That's not true," I insisted.

"Look, I saw how much he liked you back there in that car. Be honest with yourself."

"He was just mad-- that's all."

"Is that why his other girlfriend beat you up?"

"Mind your own business," I said.

"All right Niara," she said backing off.

"What are you going to do with me?" I wanted to know.

"Drive you home."

"Are you going to talk to my mother-- tell her what happened?"

"I wish I could, but I don't know what happened."

"You know enough. Are you going to tell her you found me with him?" I said pointing to Ty.

"Yes. She should know what her daughter is doing and who she is with."

"Please don't do that."

"It's part of my job."

"But she can't know that. She doesn't like Ty."

"I don't like him either."

"But I don't want her to know she was right. Not this time."

"How are you going to explain the black eyes?"

"I don't know," I admitted. "I'll have to think of something."

"You better start thinking fast," she said.

"Blake I'm finished with him," said the white officer walking up to us. "He's clean. I let him go. Are you finished here?"

"Just about, but I think we should drop her off at her house."

"I think you're right," he said looking at me.

"Come along Niara," she said.

I walked along side of the two officers. I dreaded having to explain all this to my mother. She was not going to like it at all.

"Where do you live?" the male officer asked.

"Vodges Street. 1337 South Vodges Street."

I sat back in the patrol car and waited. I felt awful. My face felt like it was four times its normal size. And I could feel every part of it throbbing. I clutched my ribs; they hurt. Even my feet hurt and I could not figure out why.

"Niara if you ever need to talk or anything-- here," said the police woman handing me a piece of paper. "It's my number. Call me anytime."

I took it and shoved it into the pocket of my jeans.

CHAPTER TWENTY THREE

"Is this it?" the white police officer asked looking at the dilapidated concrete steps. Weeds were growing through the wide crack that was dispensed evenly throughout the steps.

"Yes," I said.

I knew he was staring at the rotting porch floor. It was nothing but peeling paint and splinters.

"Can't somebody pick up a broom? People shouldn't have to live like this," said the white officer. "She shouldn't be living like this."

I shouldn't have to hear this, I thought. What did he know about how I lived? I turned my head to see what the black woman was going to say. The side of her face showed no expression, but I could not see her eyes. Didn't she hear him? I knew she did, but she didn't say a word.

The white police officer continued speaking, "It doesn't take much to keep a street clean-- a little effort, a little time-- that's all." He was noticing the mounds of trash gathering on the sidewalks in front of the narrow line of row houses.

"Colby, this is not the time-- I don't want to get into it with you."

"Why don't you shut up and mind your own business, "I said a little too softly for anyone to notice.

"This just doesn't make sense Blake and you know it. Aren't you tired of looking at this everyday? Seeing the drunks on the corners-- little dirty children running around with no

177

supervision? Doesn't anyone around here care?"

"Oh like you really care," I mumbled between swollen lips. Nobody heard me. Or, they just ignored me. I wasn't sure which it was.

"What's on my mind right now, Colby, is taking this girl home. That's what I'm concerned with. Debating and defending neighborhoods like this is not my job."

"So you don't mind seeing this all the time?" he asked.

"Don't push me-- I've seen plenty of places like this and black aren't always the ones inhabiting them either."

"I never said that-- I'm not indicting black people," he said.

"Aren't you?"

"Not at all. I would simply like to know where the adults are? Where are the parents of some of these kids? Where is this girl's mother?" he said referring to me. "How come we are the first ones to know when she gets into trouble. She's not too old to be watched. How come she's out in the street? She should be in summer camp or dance class," he paused to get air. "Where's your father?" he asked turning around to look at me. Was he searching for further ammunition to support his opinion?

"You don't know me so keep your questions to yourself," I said.

"Colby stop it!" the woman officer said in a loud tone. It was still controlled and professional, but it was becoming angry. "It's not your place to ask that. And I think you'd better keep the rest of your thoughts to yourself."

"You're right Blake," he backed down. "Let's just get this over with."

The police car was parked at the end of the block and we walked back to my house in silence. I felt like a serial killer. All the people on the street were looking at me as if I were. We reached my house and we all walked up the steps.

Who was going to knock on the door I wondered standing between them. It definitely was not going to be me. It was the black police officer who did it. No answer came. The place was quiet. She waited and then knocked again. I waited anxiously. Was my pain going away or was it being drown by nervousness.

I saw the curtain move and Cathleen's voice say, "Oh my god!"

This was not a good reaction. What was she going to do? Go off the deep end and discipline me? Or was she going to be calm and listen to my explanation? Did I have one? I didn't really know what happened. I didn't even know who the girls were that did this to me. Oh no! And what about Grandfather? Was Cathleen going to call South Carolina? Would she tell him? Oh please, please, please, God don't let her do that. He just wouldn't understand. I've never been in trouble before. He would be so disappointed in me. What were the police going to tell Cathleen? I waited. What was going to happen next?

She opened the door. Standing there in jeans and a shirt, she looked for what seemed like a long time at all of us-- especially me.

"Niara what happened to you?"

"Nothing," I said.

"I can see that's not the truth-- what's going on? She can't be in trouble?" Cathleen said disbelievingly. "She's a good kid."

"We aren't sure what went on," the black police woman

spoke up. "We got a call about a fight and we found her at the scene in this condition."

Cathleen looked back at me. "Niara have you been fighting?" she asked not believing her ears.

"No I wasn't."

"How did you get that?" she pointed at my face.

"She was not willing to tell us what happened," interjected the white police officer. "So we really don't know what happened-- but I thought it best to bring her home."

Where was all his earlier talk? The white police officer showed no animosity to this woman for being a single parent or for being a black mother. Why did he change his attitude? Was it because of the black officer next to him?

"Thank you officers for bringing her home."

I had enough. They were talking about me like I wasn't there. I pushed pass Cathleen and went in the house. Let them talk all they want; I wanted to lie down.

Going up the stairs, I passed the big mirror on the living room wall. I refused to look. I went to my room and I closed the door and hoped she wasn't going to try playing mommy again. If she did get that idea, maybe she'd loose it when she saw that my door was closed. She was the last thing I needed to deal with right now-- her or that damn dog Ty. I snatched the cord from the phone. If it got broken, I didn't care. I was too mad. Mad at Ty for treating me like a fool. Mad because I thought he was a nice guy.

I heard soft, hesitant footsteps coming up the stairs. They were slow in reaching the top. They were weak footsteps. I listened cautiously. Not now! Please don't let her come in here! I can't take this!

I listened on. I then heard those footsteps change their mind. Good. Cathleen needed to go back downstairs and mind her own business. She wasn't really concerned about me so why pretend.

"Yeah," I said. "Go on back downstairs and watch TV. Leave me alone."

I felt tears run down my face and I realized I was crying. I closed them tightly and hugged myself until I fell asleep.

When I woke up, I saw my mother sleeping in a chair across from my bed. It was a shock. Realizing she had been there all night was unimaginable. Why wasn't she at work? I noticed she had undressed me and put me to bed. The knowledge of this was warming. It gave me a nice feeling inside.

I wasn't in that bad a condition. She didn't have to sit here all night worrying about me. What made her think I was? How bad did I look? I tried to move. I felt a pain shoot through my shoulder. I tried to move my neck, but it wouldn't turn. I began to panic. I tried other parts of my body. They resisted too. Was I paralyzed? Why couldn't I move? I stopped trying after a while. I didn't want to scare myself prematurely. I didn't want to wake my mother. I didn't want her to get upset so I held all my fears in check.

I wasn't paralyzed. I was just sore-- that's all, I told myself. I wasn't going to worry about it. I tried to relax, but all I could do was stare at my mother. I waited for the aches to subside.

When I woke up the next time, it was to find Cathleen standing over me. She had a thermometer in her hand.

"Your head feels warm. Let me take your temperature."

"How long have I been sleeping?"

"Since yesterday."

I complied with her and opened my mouth. It had been sealed shut from all the hours of non-use. She stuck the instrument in and we both waited the appropriate amount of minutes it took to get an accurate reading.

She then took it out and held it up to the light. She turned it this way and then that way trying to read the thermometer.

"Ninety-nine point four. That's not that bad."

"I feel awful."

"You look even worst. I gave you a sponge bath and you're covered with purple and black marks," she said looking at me intently. Then very seriously she asked, "What happened?"

"I don't want to get into it right now."

"Did it have something to do with that boy you've been seeing--"

"I'm not sure what happened."

"He's been calling here all morning for you."

"What did you tell him?"

"That you were sleeping. I asked him if he knew who attacked you," she said as calmly as she could.

Cathleen was trying very earnestly not to push her. She was trying hard to wait and let Niara tell her what happened. Every time she pushed or bullied Niara in the past, her daughter had resisted and even refused to talk to her. She desperately wanted to know who did this to her, but she was afraid to ask too many questions.

"What did he say?"

"That he didn't know. He kept insisting that it was

182

important for him to speak to you, but I said no."

"I'm glad. I don't ever want to talk to him again. Not after yesterday--" I said, stopping myself when I realized what else I was about to say.

I did not want to admit anything to Cathleen right now. I did not want to admit Ty's girlfriend was the one who did this to me.

"You can tell me anything Niara-- I've done too much in my own life to be too judgmental."

"It's nothing really. I just got into a stupid fight-- that's all. It's no big deal."

"You look pretty beat up for it to be no big deal," she said gently. "I'll get the Tylenol for you," she left the room.

She came back carrying a glass of water and two tablets. "Take this."

"Thanks," I said reaching out and taking them from her. I gulped them down with warm water and then handed her back the glass.

"I think you should stay in bed until the swelling on your face goes down. You are going to need to take it easy."

"I'm too sore to even get out of bed," I said smiling slightly.

"I took off from the hospital for a couple of nights," she informed me.

"You shouldn't have done that."

"I got lots of sick time. Besides I just want to make sure I don't have to take you to the hospital. It doesn't look serious, but I want to be sure."

"Okay," I said lying back down on the pillow. No sooner

had my head touched it than I fell back to sleep.

CHAPTER TWENTY FOUR

I stood in front of the bathroom mirror. I tried to see my image, but the steam made it impossible. It hid all the blue-purple swelling that layered my entire face. I was glad I couldn't see it because I would start crying. Was my face ever going to look normal?

I packed my face in ice; I used loads and loads of cocoa butter; I took cold baths-- hot baths, but nothing was helping. How long was I going to look like this?

I took off all my clothes and stepped into the hot tub of water-- very slowly. First one foot, then the other-- gradually I eased my whole body into it. I relaxed in it and sat quietly listening to the dripping of the sink. I did not care how long I sat in the tub. This was the one place where I was guaranteed privacy. No Ty. No Cathleen. Just quietness.

As I noticed the water getting cooler, I took a deep breath and slid under its foamed surface. My hair floated in it and the slightest movement of water massaged my tender face. It felt good. My ears filled with water and bubbles; they felt like earplugs, but that did not keep out my mother's voice.

"Niara!" I jumped. "Are you in there?"

I didn't answer her, but waited until I needed oxygen. I then pushed myself up in the tub.

"Yes," I waited.

"Telephone," she said.

"Who is it?"

"Kelli. She says it's important."

"Tell her I'll talk to her at work."

Cathleen did not reply, but I heard her walking away from the door.

Today was going to be my first day back to work since the fight. I had been trapped inside this house for a week. I needed out. In here, I had too much time to think about Ty and the mistakes I made. I didn't want to think about either anymore. I was tired of dwelling on them.

Ty called me again this morning; he wanted to see me. He said he missed me. He could miss me all he wanted. I didn't want anything to do with him. I never wanted to talk to him again. I told him so and then hung up the phone. The phone immediately began ringing again, but I wouldn't answer it.

Whatever feelings I had for him were gone. They went away the very moment I found out about his girlfriend. How could he be seeing me and that girl at the same time? How could he do that to me? I hated his guts. How could he do it? I thought he liked me. I thought I was somebody special. I was no different to him than that other girl. He was lying to us both. No, I definitely had nothing more to say to him. We were through.

I thought once more about the afternoon of the fight. Was the black policewoman right? She said I was just being used-- that I fit a profile-- that if I wasn't pretty, I wouldn't be getting the time of day from somebody like Ty. That thought hurt. It made me feel like a piece of furniture, like I had no real worth. Did he have me on display? Was I supposed to be something all his friends were to admire? Was he only seeing me because I made him look good. I thought he liked me! I thought he really cared about me! I guess I

186

was wrong.

I felt angry. I felt stupid, dumb. What he did to me was wrong. He chose me for my looks. He didn't choose me because I was a nice person-- I stopped dead in my thoughts. I didn't want to admit it but I realized unwillingly that he did exactly the same thing I did. The only reason I agreed to go out with him was because I thought he was cute. I didn't know anything about him. I didn't know what kind of person he was. I didn't even know if he finished high school or if he had any hobbies. I knew nothing about him except that he was handsome and black.

I chose him for all the wrong reasons, I thought easing out of the water. I chose him because I liked the way he talked-- the way he made me feel. I liked him because he was older than me. Because I thought he was mature-- those were all the wrong reasons for jumping into a relationship.

I carefully dried myself and then my hair. I pulled on a towel robe. I picked up my dirty clothes and threw them into the hamper.

I didn't feel like cleaning out the tub, but I did it anyway. I thought about the first time I used it and laughed aloud. Cathleen had been furious with me for leaving it dirty and when I got home she made sure I knew it.

I walked back to my room and looked at the clock. If I didn't want to be late, I'd better hurry up and get dressed. I was supposed to be at Turner's mini-market in an hour.

CHAPTER TWENTY FIVE

"How long are you going to keep this up-- huh?" Tyress remarked cornering me in the canned vegetable aisle.

I wasn't working register today; Mr. Turner thought I should take it easy on my first day back. He suggested that I price and restock the shelves.

"How long do you plan on ignoring me?" Ty continued.

"I'm not ignoring you," I said pretending to be calm, but I didn't want him here.

"No? So why don't you take any of my phone calls?"

"Because I have nothing to say to you."

"You have nothing to say to me," he mimicked. "Since when?"

"Since I found out you had a girlfriend."

"Ex," he corrected.

"She wasn't acting like nobody's ex," I challenged.

"Well that's all she is."

"Whatever you say."

"That's how it is," he said. "And don't go blamin' me for what happened. I didn't know she was gonna get like that-- I tried to break it up."

"I'm tired of this Ty. Stop calling me. And stop bothering me. I know you were seeing her and me at the same time-- I heard her say it. So just leave me alone, will you?"

"Stop acting like a baby and listen to me-- she was lying."

"You can say what you want, but I know different."

"So what are you saying? It's over? Just like that, we're through?"

"Yes," I said. "I don't want a boyfriend anymore. I'm too young for all this stuff-- sex, jealous girlfriends-- you," I said trailing off into silence.

"Let me take you out tonight," he suggested. "I think we need to do some serious talking."

"I got work to do Ty," I said moving away from him.

"I'm not finished," he said grabbing me by the arm. "Don't try treatin' me like some little boy you can boss around. I won't go for that. I said we needed to talk."

"Get off of me," I said trying to yank away, but I couldn't. His grip was too firm.

"You are my girl and that's the way it's gonna be until I say different. I ain't gonna let some silly fight change things between us."

"I'm not your girl," I said uneasily. "Not anymore."

"Don't play games with me Niara."

"I'm not," I said in a frightened, pleading voice.

"I want to see you tonight, after work."

"I can't--"

The imprisonment of my arm by his strong black hands bound me to him. I could not move until he decided I should. Maybe I should agree to meet him-- agree to anything just to get away from him. My fears were beginning to mount. I had not expected him to react like this when I made the decision not to see him again. What was I going to do now?

If it had not been for the change of expression on Ty's face, I would not have known someone was walking up behind us. I turned to see who it was.

"What's going on here?" I heard Mr. Turner's voice. "Let her go."

"I'm simply talking to Niara," said Ty.

"You don't need your hands to do that," responded Mr. Turner.

"Are you all right Niara?"

"Yes."

"You didn't answer me Ty. Why are you handling her like that?"

"This here is between her and me, Sam," he said deliberately using the older man's first name as a display of disrespect.

"Not in here. And I don't want you harassing her anymore--"

"Who is this guy?" demanded Ty of me. "He don't know nothing about me so why is he approaching me like he does?"

"Please leave," I said wanting Ty to stop all this commotion.

"Have you been talking to this guy about us? Have you?" he asked getting angrier. "What have you told him?"

"I-- I only told him what happened."

"And what was that?"

"About the fight."

"Oh you told him that," said Ty sarcastically. "Did you also tell him the other stuff? Did you tell him about all them nights you snuck out of the house just to be with me? Did you tell him about the passion mark I put on you right there?" he asked reaching out and touching me softly on my lower neck.

"Please-- don't do that," I said.

"And did you tell him how much you liked it? By the look on your face, I guess not. Look here Sam, you don't know everything that's going on between us so why don't you just back off. This don't concern you."

"I want you to leave. She is a little girl-- find somebody your own age."

"What if I won't go? You're a little too old to be getting physical, Sam," he said standing his ground. "What if I don't want to walk out that door?"

"Then there is going to be a confrontation."

"Is it like that Sam? You really want to fight me? I am three times your age, old man."

"Maybe so, but I want you to go."

"I ain't afraid of you," he said retreating a little from the older man. "I was just about finished here anyway."

"Good," said Mr. Turner.

"This ain't over Niara. Next time it's just gonna be you and me--" he said pointing in my direction and then at himself. "And I tell you now things are gonna be happening."

I watched him retreat further down the aisle and eventually out of the store, but I still could not control the trembling that was reverberating throughout my body. What did he mean by 'next time'? There wasn't going to be a next time. I was not going anywhere he was. Why couldn't he just leave me alone?

"Thanks," I said.

"You're not still seeing him Niara?" asked Mr. Turner.

"No. That's why he came here."

"Does your mother know he's threatening you?"

"Not really. I don't want her worrying about me. He's not going to do nothing."

"You can't be sure of that. The boy just threatened you. She should be aware of it."

"He didn't mean it," I said, not even believing the words myself.

"We don't know that. Tell your mother Niara. Don't keep this to yourself."

"I don't know," I said picking up the pricing gun. I needed something to do with my hands. They were trembling out of control.

"Why him Niara?" he asked handing me a can of peas. "What made you choose him?"

"I don't want to talk about it. I feel stupid about the whole thing now."

"I'd like to know. You're a smart girl-- what was your reason?"

"Because he was cute," I said feeling even dumber now that the words were out. "I didn't plan for any of this to happen. It just did."

"You are way too young to be going out with boys. And sneaking out at night with any boy is not the mature thing to do. You shouldn't be sneaking out with anybody. You need to wait until you are a woman before you begin a relationship. It's all right to like a boy. Or even have a friend that is a boy, but that should be it. I'm not scolding you, but this is what's wrong with so many people today-- including me. I had my first relationship when I was too, too young. People got to take it slow. My mistake was that when I was your age I didn't take it slow either. My mind wasn't on friendship. Or trying to figure out who I was as an individual. Or what I wanted for my future. Or what kind of a woman I wanted to share it with. Instead, all I wanted to do was get alone with a girl and do things I had no business doing-- we didn't have sex, but it came damn close. And we both ended up getting our feelings hurt. She thought I was in love with her, but I wasn't. I thought that I was establishing my manhood. But I wasn't. I know that now. Protecting your children's future by not having babies before you are able to nurture them or teach them or provide for them is establishing your manhood. I know respecting a girl until she becomes a woman is doing that.

"I know what I did was wrong," I said.

" But do you know why it was wrong?"

"I think so."

"Why?"

"I know kissing and touching-- and being alone all the time can lead to other things. Things I'm not going to want to do right now. Things I might not want to do until I become an adult. And I guess, I should've thought about that before I started seeing Ty."

"You are right. Your future is more important than an encounter with a boy. And looks don't always tell the truth about a person."

"I know that now," I said.

"This may not be my place Niara, but I'm simply asking because I want to make sure this hasn't been overlooked by your people."

"What?" I said looking at him.

193

"Has anyone talked to you about-- sex?"

"Of course," I said nervously. "I know what I need to know-- about babies, and stuff."

"I'm glad you know about 'babies, and stuff'," he said a little playfully. "Does the 'and stuff' mean contraceptives?"

"Yes," I mumbled looking down.

"Good, but has anybody talked to you about the feelings that come along with having sex?"

"No," I said quietly.

He took a long paused before he continued speaking, "The first time you have sex it is going to be painful."

"I know," I said shyly. "You don't really need to do this."

"I think you need to hear this. Just let me finish."

I closed my mouth.

"Your body needs to adjust to the new experience. It could take years before your body completely adjusts."

"Years!" I repeated startled by his remarks.

"It depends on the person-- and I'm not saying you won't find it enjoyable. You will. But what I am saying is that loving and respecting the person you are having sex with will make that temporary physical transition exciting and memorable."

"I'm going to wait," I said.

"I know, but I guess what I'm trying to tell you is why you should wait. Experimenting with sex is just going to complicate your life-- sleeping with boys is going to have you always comparing them and what you did with them to any future partner."

I continued to stare at the floor, but I listened to him.

"Too many girls find it hard to trust guys after they've had

194

sex with them and then the boy leaves-- don't put yourself in that position."

"I won't," I said softly.

"Virginity and innocence are the sweetest things you can offer your husband and it is the most precious gift he can give to you."

"How do you know so much? Were you married before?"

"Yes, but she died in a car accident four years ago," he got extremely quiet and reflective for a moment.

"Your wife, was she a virgin?"

"Yes. And she taught me so much about sex and trust and love. That's how I know it can be more than just a physical action."

"I want that when I get married," I said.

"You'll get it. Just make sure you take your time choosing that person," he said handing me the last can of peas.

"Thanks Mr. Turner."

"I'm glad you listened," he said.

CHAPTER TWENTY SIX

Even though, Mr. Turner walked me to my house, I didn't truly feel safe until I put my key in the door and pushed it opened. I expected Ty to be waiting for me in every obscure doorway or on every corner we passed. But he wasn't. I tried to calm myself and think about what I'd do when I got home. Maybe I'd call Grandfather; I hadn't written to him in over two weeks. He'd be surprised to hear from me. Yes, that's what I'd do.

We made it passed all the suspicious dark spots and quiet streets. I said goodnight to Mr. Turner as I walked up the steps.

"Thank you God," I whispered closing the door behind me.

I needed noise. The house was too quiet. I turned on the radio. The jumping, loud music made me feel better. Cathleen was at work, but I was glad she left the hall light on upstairs. It made the house less intimidating.

I smelt the odor of perfectly fried chicken coming from the kitchen. Usually when people fried chicken the last pieces cooked were always burnt; this was because the flames were too high and the oil by this time was black. But Cathleen knew better. Hers was always just right. My stomach began to growl; its hunger was reawakened. I could go for a drumstick smothered in hot sauce, I thought walking toward the kitchen.

As I moved through the dark dinning room, I heard a crunching noise beneath my feet. What was that? I strained my eyes to identify what I was walking on-- what was making that shearing sound. I reached for the light switch and flipped it up.

Why was there broken glass all over the floor? Where had it come from? Following the trail slowly with my eyes, it led to our dinning room window. Instinctively I pushed the curtain aside and felt something sharp scrape my hand. I quickly drew it back. Hesitantly, I reached out again and this time I pushed it further aside. The window had been smashed. Who would do this? A fear washed over me, drenching me in a hot frightened sweat. Was someone in the house?

I let the curtain drop. I began backing away from the window. I was afraid to take my eyes off the swinging curtain. It swished back and forth hypnotizing me.

"Sorry 'bout the window," a voice said behind my left ear.

I let out a scream and straightened up immediately. I tried to turn around, but he walked right into my back causing me to move forward in order to evade his body.

I tried to moved away from him, but he continued to push further into my back until I had nowhere to go. He walked me into a dining room wall.

"Why are you doing this?"

"Ain't you glad to see me baby?" he said moving closer. "Or did you think after what happened in the store today, I'd just disappear?"

"Why can't you leave me alone?" I asked softly, trying not to cry. I felt my eyes getting watery.

"'cause I came to get what's mine."

"What's that supposed to mean?"

'That you owe me something," he said, grabbing me lightly by the throat. The grasp didn't hurt but I did not like the way he did it or what he was saying.

"I-- I owe you nothing," I said trying to move away from him.

"Yes you do girl. You owe me a lot-- and I want it now."

"No I don't."

"The hell you don't. You ain't gonna tease me for months and then think you can walk away like you didn't do a thing. It ain't like that."

"I wasn't teasing you."

"Seemed like it to me. All that grinding we did and I never got no sex. That's teasing to me."

Please let me go," I repeated.

"Not until we finish things,' he said smiling.

"Why are you doing this?"

"How else am I gonna talk to you? You keep ignoring my phone calls-- and now you got your boss kicking me out of his store. This is the only way I can get to you."

"Please leave," I said trying to push him. "I never said I was going to have sex with you. If you thought that, it's not my fault--"

"Ain't you something," he said keeping his hands on my neck. "You never used to talk like that to me. Is this more of your new attitude? Because if it is, I don't like it."

"Why don't you just leave?"

"I don't feel like it."

"I don't have time for this--" I began saying when I felt his hands move from around my neck; they began pulling my shirt from the waist of my jeans.

"Stop it!" I yelled. I got very panicky. Was he going to try to rape me?

"Don't do this!" I tried to push his hands away.

"Why? You got some other nigger in mind?" he asked sarcastically.

"No. Because I'm a virgin," I said faintly.

"Stop lying. Virgins don't act like you've been acting."

"I'm not lying," I said trying to get from between him and the dinning room wall.

"It doesn't matter," he said, undoing my zipper.

He yanked my jeans down to my hips. His movement wasn't gentle. I could feel the rough material of my jeans scraping against my legs-- probably leaving streaks of red bruises where my jeans had been.

His next action was even more violent. He pulled my shirt apart; I did not hear any buttons fall to the floor so I guess the manufacturer had sown them on very securely.

"Damn! Don't you look good."

"Ty this isn't right-- you've been drinking. I can smell it."

"So what's that got to do with anything?"

"You wouldn't be acting like this if--"

"I'm not drunk-- just had a few beers, that's all. But you know what isn't right?" he asked.

"What?"

"That you've been keeping this pretty body from me all this time," he said smashing his hands into my breasts. Was that supposed to be a caress? It felt more like a punch.

"You can't do this-- I won't let you."

"What are you gonna do to stop me?" he asked.

What could I do? I could scream, but would anybody hear me? And if they did, would they call 911? Around here screaming was not that unusual and many times people ignored it. Their attitude was why get involved in somebody else's business. If the person crying out for help got himself into it, he could damn sure get himself out of it. I could fight back, but he was too strong. What the hell was I going to do?

I had to pee badly. My mind kept screaming it, but I couldn't move. He wouldn't let me. Suddenly, I felt hot urine run down my legs. It streamed into my sneakers and gradually turned cold.

"I have to use the bathroom," I said belatedly.

"You know where it is," he stated.

"I can just go?"

"Go ahead."

"You're not going to stop me?"

"Why should I?"

"I'll be right back," I said.

I was surprised he allowed me to break away from him. Maybe he wasn't going to try anything. Maybe he was bluffing. If he was, this wasn't funny. I walked pass him and half ran for the staircase.

As I moved, I heard him say, "Got to use it myself. Lead the way."

He was walking behind me. Following me up the stairs. I got to do something! I got to get away from him! When I reached the top step, I bolted toward the bathroom. I ran not paying attention to the hamper in the hallway. I bumped into it, but it didn't slow me down. Neither did the plastic trash bag outside the bathroom door.

"Girl you can't outrun me," I heard him say as he began

running behind me. "I've outrun niggers running from the cops-- so you ain't nothing."

I've got to get to the bathroom! I can't let him stop me! I picked up my feet and ran faster. I wasn't going to let him rape me in my own house! I had to make it to the bathroom. I could not afford to let him beat me to it. I thought I was going to reach it. I almost did, but then I felt two hands grabbing my shirt and pulling me backward. I ran even faster, but I wasn't getting anywhere. He was controlling my every movement.

"You think I'm that dumb-- you think I'm gonna just let you lock yourself in there all night-- girl I've been around longer than that."

"Get off of me!" I screamed. This time I didn't care if the neighbors would responded to it or not. I was desperate. "You can't rape me!"

"Who said I was going to do that?"

"Help--" I tried to scream. I could feel him pulling me down and pinning me to the hallway floor. As I struggled, I felt the rug burning my neck and shoulders. My shirt must have gotten hiked up in all the activity.

"You've been begging for this for a long time," he said.

"No!" I bit into his neck; it tasted rubbery-- nothing like what I expected skin to taste like.

"You bit me! Dumb bitc--" he uttered releasing my body from his imprisoning hands. His hands then encased the sides of my face, stopping the circulation of blood from making its way through that part of my body. The scream I was going to release froze in my throat. I could tell he was going to hit me long before the actual punch came. I received it in the mouth. I thought I

201

heard my front teeth pop out. Did he hit me that hard? I felt my lips exploding like an air bag being released upon full impact.

Why didn't I taste blood? I slid my tongue around my mouth expecting to feel two empty sockets where my teeth should have been. What I felt instead were two smooth teeth. I didn't have time to feel relief; Ty hit me again. But this time it was my jaw that received his impact. My face and neck did not resist his blow, but followed it out to completion.

"I never did anything to you--" I tried saying, but some of the words got lost. I was having trouble speaking.

"Relax baby, this ain't gonna hurt," he promised.

"Help! Anybody-- help!"

"You ain't gonna need help-- all I'm about to do is make you feel good."

"Get off!" I bellowed, my hands clawing at his shirt and arms. "I can't let this happen!" I shouted, hysteria evident in my every word. I fought Ty from that moment on the same way I would any demon in a horror movie. I fought like all my tomorrows were in jeopardy. And in fact they were. If he raped me, I would never be the same again. I punched him, kicked him, bit him. Whatever came to mind I did. I raked my fingernails against his eyes trying to blind him. We looked like a human ball rolling around on the floor. And he fought me as vigorously as I fought him.

As we continued to maul each other on the floor, I suddenly noticed a change in myself. I was breathing harder. It was heavier and faster than before. I was lying on him-- resting on him-- trying to catch my breath. What was happening to me?

My fingernails were desperately trying to accumulate

brown skin underneath their hard enamel, but I wasn't succeeding. If I was accumulating anything, it was threads and fibers from his shirt.

"Niara you might as well give it up. Because you can't beat me. Don't you know that?"

No I didn't realize that-- all I knew was that I had to get away. I had to fight until I couldn't do it anymore. I had to get out of here. That's all I knew.

But things were moving too fast, he was moving too fast. Ty was ripping and pulling at my clothes. He was trying to get my jeans off.

No! I can't give up! I can't let him win! I tried to fight him-- hoping my kicks dug into his legs, thighs, stomach, and if I was lucky his penis.

I didn't know as we fought we were inching toward the stairs. All I was aware of was his hands touching my body-- trying to rip my clothes off me. So when we felt the thumping of our bodies' against the hard steps, we both let out sounds of astonishment. Mine fearful, his surprised. Our bodies crashed against one another and rolled over top of each other. We picked up momentum with the continuing fall. We did not stop gathering speed until we broke through the wooden railing. Its splintering sound rung in my ears. I laid there bruised, and numb. It didn't take me long to recover from my fall. I looked for Ty. He was less than a foot away from me and unmoving. I stood there. Was he all right? I wanted to move closer, but I couldn't. Then I heard a slight moan escape his lips. That was all it took to send me running for the front door. If he got up, I wasn't aware of it. I ran frantically. If I could make it to the avenue, I would be safe. I half ran half fell through the front door and into the street. I could not scream and run so I simply ran.

I listened for someone following me, but I didn't turn around to see if that was the case. I ran toward the main avenue. I was afraid of any small street or alleyway.

The air cut into my eyes as I ran; they began to tear. I ran harder. When I reached Chester Avenue, I ran wildly into the street. I saw lots of people, but I still ran. I didn't feel safe. I ran and ran and ran until I had no choice but to stop. And that was when, I stumbled onto cement steps on some street I didn't recognize. I collapsed against them and cried.

My mouth was dry. I didn't realize it was because I'd ran with it open for two blocks. I let my head rest against the hard steps, and closed my eyes and continued to breath heavily. I didn't know if Ty was behind me-- I simply had to rest. I wanted to hide in the bushes across the street, but my body made me resist the urge.

"Phone-- I got to get to a phone," I panted.

I pulled myself up from the steps and looked up and down the street for a pay phone. I saw one a block away.

"Are you all right Miss?" a black man asked hesitantly.

As the man asked the question, I realized at once that my shirt was open.

"You want me to get the police?"

"No-- I'm all right," I managed to get out as I moved pass him and made my way to the telephone.

I didn't have money! I left it at the house. What was I going to do? These questions rushed at me as I picked up the receiver. I could not stay here all night. I pushed zero, and waited

for the operator's voice. When I heard it, I felt relief and spoke.
"Can-- I make a collect call?"
"Hang up, dial zero and then the number you want to reach," the operator said.
"I'm not sure about the number."
"Dial information. That number is 555-1212."
"But I don't have any money Miss," my voice was panic stricken.
"Do you know the full name of the party you are trying to reach?"
"Yes. I want to reach C. R. Drew Hospital-- the chemistry lab," I said.
"Hold on please," there was a pause. "I cannot get that number. Do you want me to dial the main number?"
"Yes."
The operator said, "In case we get disconnected the number is 827-3556."
There was another pause and then the operator returned to the phone. "I'm sorry, but they won't accept the charges."
"But they have to! It's an emergency."
"I would like to help you, but I cannot do anything else. I'm sorry."
"Thanks," I put down the phone.
What was I going to do now? I needed thirty-five cents. I could not continue walking around like this.
I saw a man standing on the corner in front of a bar. I could ask him, but I did not like the idea. I did not want to put myself in an awkward position.
I saw a woman walking with her son.

"Could I have thirty-five cents--" I begged.

She looked at me and ignored me, "Come on Dimitrius. We got crack addicts everywhere."

"I'm not on crack!" I shouted at her.

"Girl you better go on about your business before you get hurt," she threatened.

I saw another woman walking down the street. I felt very uncomfortable asking her.

"Please Miss-- I need some money to make a phone call," I said in a rushed sentence. I didn't want her to say no too. "I was almost raped and I need to call my mother-- please."

She looked shocked. "Yes I got it," she said digging around in her purse until she pulled out several coins.

"You want me to get the police?"

"No-- I just want to call my mother. She will know what to do--" I took the money. "Thank you," I said walking, half running to the phone.

In one swift movement, I deposited the money and dialed the main number to the hospital. I got the operator.

"Can I speak to Miss Saunders?"

"Is she a patient?"

"No-- she works in the chemistry lab."

"Please hold."

I waited for the call to go through. There was a silent pause and then I heard, "Chemistry laboratory, may I help you?"

"Mom! It's me!"

"Niara? What's going on?"

"-- could you come get me?"

"Why? What's going on Niara? Are you in trouble?"

"I need you to come get me," I repeated.

"What happened?"

"I-- I came home from work-- and he was there."

"Who?"

"I didn't know he was going to act like that--" I began crying.

"Niara! Niara! What's going on? Where are you?"

"Divine Street--" I said glancing up at the street sign. "I'm scared."

"Was it Ty? Did he do something to you?" I could hear the terror building in Cathleen's voice.

"He tried to rape me," I was crying hysterically now.

"Please God no!" Cathleen prayed. "I'm coming to get you-- I'll be right there."

"I need a shirt. He ripped it--"

"I'm coming Niara. Are-- you sure he didn't rape you?" she asked in a weak voice.

"Hurry."

"You're at what in Divine?"

"54th-- across the street from a bar."

"Give me twenty minutes."

"Wait Mom," I said and paused.

"Yes?"

"I'm sorry for this-- for everything."

"I'm on my way," I heard her say and then she hung up.

CHAPTER TWENTY SEVEN

The 139th precinct was crowded; probably just like every other police station in this city. There were all kinds of people there, but most of them were young men and all of them were black. This fact became blatantly obvious to me once my mother and I entered the small building.

I pulled the ripped shirt tighter to my body and wondered why I was allowing Cathleen to bring me here. This was not what I wanted to do. I didn't want to have him arrested; I just wanted him to leave me alone. I wanted to go home; I wanted to forget, but I allowed my mother to lead me further into the precinct.

Cathleen walked up to a glass window separating us from the police officers. She waited for someone to notice her. She waited, and waited until a white officer did.

"My daughter was attacked. And I want to have something done about it."

The man looked at her and then me, "What happened?" there was no concern in his voice, his tone was routine. He was numb to her situation and simply proceeded because it was his duty.

I said nothing.

"Do you know who did this to you?" he asked.

No answer.

"Was it your boyfriend?"

"She doesn't have a boyfriend," my mother jumped in defensively.

"Where did it happen?"

I couldn't answer him. I looked down at the floor.

"Were you raped?"

"No!" I yelled.

"Who was it," he repeated.

Silence.

"Was it a friend?"

No answer.

"How old are you?" he inquired impatiently.

No answer. I was tired of that question. Why was it, whenever something important happened to me everybody always wanted to know my age? Was that going to change the significance of what happened to me?

"She's sixteen."

"Her name?" he began filling out a form.

"Niara Saunders," my mother answered.

"Address?"

"1337 South Vodges Street."

These questions continued and Cathleen obediently answered them giving all the appropriate information. But eventually it became my turn to speak.

"Was it one person or more?"

No answer.

"Did you know him?"

No answer.

"Are you sure you weren't raped?" the officer demanded.

No answer.

"What's his name?"

No answer.

"Where were you when it happened?"

"She was at home," Cathleen broke in. "Come on Niara. Tell him something."

I continued to look down at the floor. My mouth would not open nor begin speaking. Whether it was right or wrong, I didn't want to tell anyone. I felt embarrassed. What was I supposed to say-- this boy who I thought I liked broke into my house and tried to rape me-- only I got away because-- I don't even really know why I got away!

"Look," said the police officer. "Unless you tell me something, there is nothing I can do for you or your mother."

No answer.

"It was a boy named Ty," said Cathleen.

"Are you sure?" he asked.

"Yes. He's the only boy my daughter has been seeing."

"Did she tell you it was him?"

"No, but--"

"I need facts. I can't pick somebody up simply because they dated your daughter. She has to tell me what happened," he said looking at me.

"Tell the man Niara. Don't protect him. What he did was wrong. You got to tell us what happened-- don't be ashamed. It wasn't your fault."

No answer.

"Why don't you take her home. If she changes her mind tomorrow, we will still be able to fill out a report."

"No! I want something done tonight. I don't want him walking around on the streets. The next time he might rape her. First she gets beat up because of him and now this. I want him picked up!"

"We can't do anything until she talks. And I don't think that's going to happen."

"Niara honey," pleaded Cathleen. "Tell us who it was. Let me be your mother again. Trust me-- let me help you. Was it Ty?"

No answer.

"I love you Niara-- and I don't want this to happen again. Let us help you-- was it him?"

I searched her face. I wanted Cathleen to make everything all right. I wanted to be protected. I wanted to be a daughter. And I wanted her to be my mother. I wanted this summer to start all over again, because I had done so many things wrong. I should have been nicer to my mother and I should have stayed away from Ty.

But that couldn't happen so all I could do was deal with the choices I had made.

"Yes," I murmured in a tiny voice.

CHAPTER TWENTY EIGHT

I DIDN'T OPEN MY EYES until I felt the car stop. I forced myself to sit up and look out of the window. I did not want to go back into that house. I did not want to walk up those front steps. I did not want to go through that doorway. I did not want to remember. I could hear my screams. I could taste the fear on my lips. My body began to tremble. I looked up, and saw my mother staring at me through the rearview mirror. Her eyes searched mine.

"Do you want to sit here for a minute?"

"Yes."

"I'll lock the doors."

As she spoke, she reached out and manually locked each one. Under different circumstances, I would have laughed at her actions; this car was too obsolete. In another year or too, the city would be forced to condemn it.

I continued to stare out of the window. I watched the two policemen step onto the pavement. They were waiting for my mother.

I heard Cathleen slam the driver's door. She approached the men and spoke quietly to them. After several minutes, the men left her side and cautiously mounted the front steps.

One officer yelled, "Police!" and entered the house.

The second followed his lead.

Cathleen didn't move. She peered up at the dark house and waited. That's all either of us could do.

What would the police find?

Was he still inside? Unconscious? Dead?

I couldn't stop all the questions that ran through my head. Or, had he been behind my when I ran out of the house?

My head began to throb. It pounded, and ached. The pain began to build. I closed my eyes and tried to forget. This whole night was unreal.

He tried to rape me!

Why?

In one summer so much had happened. I couldn't comprehend it all. My grandmother died. My mother showed up from nowhere. And now this--

"Niara."

"Huh?"

"We can go inside. He's not there."

I pulled up the knob, and opened the door. I saw the police pull off, "Are you sure?"

"They searched the whole hous--"

"Even the basement?"

"Yes. He's gone."

"I'm still scared," I admitted.

"He's not coming back Niara."

"What about the broken window? He could get in through there."

"The police helped me board it up."

"I didn't see you go inside," I said confused. Had I fallen asleep?

"I waited until they said it was safe."

"Oh," I acknowledged, looking up at the house. Now all the lights were on. The house seemed to glow. It still did not look inviting. It reminded me of a haunted house. I shuddered. How was I going to go back inside? My mother must have read my thoughts, "Do you want to sit here a little longer?"

"Please."

"That's fine Niara-- there's no rush. When you're ready, we can go inside."

I slid over and made room for her. She said nothing, but got inside and shut the door. I leaned back against the seat and closed my eyes. My mind was still active. It kept replaying the attack inside my head-- over and over again.

One minute turned into ten. And ten into twenty-- and slowly I began to relax. I turned my head sideways and opened my eyes. I looked at my mother. She was also deep in thought. Her face creased, eyes focused on the seat in front of her.

"I don't want to leave," my words startled her. "Not until the end of the summer."

"We'll talk about it in the morning."

"I won't change my mind," there was a stubborn tone in my voice. "I want to have a mother," I repeated quietly.

"And I want a daughter-- but I cannot let anything happen to you--," her voice cracked. She stopped, tried to pull herself together and continued, "He might try this again."

"I'm scared, but I can't leave now," I started talking real fast. " I can stay over Kelli's house while you're at work. Or, I can--"

"No," said Cathleen.

"But what if--," I trailed off. I needed to be with my mother. But how could I convince her? I was just as afraid as she was. I didn't know whether Ty would come back.

"Do you really want me in your life?" she asked.

"Of course-- too much has happened for you not to be. And we've both changed a lot. Haven't we?" I searched her face for reassurance.

"Yes we have," smiled Cathleen. Then she said, "I'll take some time off. See how things go."

"Can you?"

"Yes," she smiled even harder. "You are very important to me. And despite all that's happened. I have never stopped loving you."

I tried to speak, but what could I say. It felt good to know she cared about me. She was a woman I didn't know, but wanted to.

"I'm ready to go inside," I stated.

"Good," she said and gave me a hug. "Things will get better. And one day, you will meet a nice young man."

"I can wait," I said. "I'm in no hurry right now."

"I know, but all men are not like the one you met this summer. Some are kind. Considerate. Loving."

"Have you met any?" I asked honestly.

"Yes."

"Who?" I asked leaning closer to her. I was comfortable resting in the curve of her arm. "Whooooo," I repeated.

"A man at work."

"And?"

"And I don't know what's going to happen, but he is respectful-- "

"Do you like him?"

"Maybe."

215

"Do you?" I demanded.

"A little," she conceded

"So where is he? I've never met him."

"Stop with the questions. The point to all this is, there are fine young men out here. You just have to take your time. See where they're coming from. And pick carefully."

"I hear you," I said.

"I'm glad," she said reaching for the door handle.

CHAPTER TWENTY NINE

"Arc you going to miss mc?" Kclli askcd.

"Nooooooooo," I smiled.

"You won't forget all about me once you get back home?

"Nope," I said.

"And you will call me?" she persisted

"Every chance I get."

"Are you sure?"

"Yes," I said for the umpteenth time.

For one week, that's all Kelli and I talked about. I did not want to leave, but I missed my Grandfather. And I was ready to return to school. I was now in the eleventh grade. And for some reason, I couldn't wait to do all the things promised to me. This year I would take my class picture. Look at school rings. Go to my Junior Prom. Decide where I wanted to go to college-- visit campuses. Fill out applications. Even take the SAT's.

I didn't look forward to that, but it came with the year. This was going to be my year. A surge of electrical excitement erupted in my stomach and traveled disruptively throughout my limbs.

I couldn't wait.

I heard Kelli talking behind me. We were in my room. She was sitting on the edge of the bed watching me pack. I didn't have a lot to pack since most of my things had stayed in the boxes. But what little I had, I arranged in my suitcase neatly.

"And if anything serious happens?" Kelli continued.

217

" I'll call you one second after it occurs."

"All right," she conceded.

"And the same thing goes for you," I said.

"You know it," she smiled.

"Hand me those books on the dresser," I asked deciding to make Kelli work.

She gave me a funny looked, but got up from the bed, "I told you once. I ain't helping you pack. So don't ask me to do nothing else."

"I hear you," I said. Kelli had already declared she did not want me to leave. And promised not to help me in any way. So I wasn't going to push it.

"Did Najee leave yet?"

"Yep."

"How do you feel about that?" I asked looking under the bed for something I might have forgotten.

"Lonely," said Kelli.

"With me around?"

"You don't play basketball."

"I could learn."

"It still wouldn't be the same." she said.

"I know. I'm not tall, dark, and athletic--," then I paused looking closely at Kelli. "You really do like him, huh?"

"He's nice. Before he left for school, he asked me and my mother over to his house for a Sunday dinner. Do you believe that? I didn't know people still did that kind of stuff."

"Impressive," I acknowledged.

"What did your mom say when you told her?"

Kelli screwed up her lips and mimicked her mother, "I ain't

settin' foot in nobody's house this coming Sunday. I'm gonna go
to the casinos. Already got my ticket."

"She didn't go to Atlantic City?" I asked dumbfounded.

"Yes she did. Got right on that bus. And took off for A C
Didn't even miss a heartbeat."

I shook my head, "She's wild."

"You got that right. I knew she wouldn't come. The one
time it really meant a lot to me--" she trailed off.

"Did his family understand?"

"I guess so. I told them she had something important to do-
- what else could I do?" she said searching my face.

"Nothing else," I said.

"But my little brother came along-- ate like a pig," she
smiled broadly. Her teeth were even, white and perfect. She was a
very pretty girl. Niara admired her best friend.

"What'd they have?"

"Everything. I can't blame my brother-- we had potato
salad. Collard greens and turnips mixed with smoked turkey.
Stuffed cornish hens. Candied yams. Pasta salad with shrimp--"

"You can stop Kelli!" I screamed. "You're making me
hungry," I said rubbing my stomach."

"It was great," she beamed.

"And his mother?"

"She was real friendly. Treated me nice-- not like I was
some girl out to hurt her son. I think I like her."

"-- and your brother?"

"Oh he liked everybody and everything. I couldn't keep
him away from their cats. One was named Blue Panther. And the
other, Zeus. Weird names, huh?"

I nodded my head.

"Anyway my little brother couldn't keep his hands off them. And I couldn't help but wish that night would never end," she said dreamily.

"I bet you couldn't" I said.

For the rest of that night, I stayed in my room and listened to Kelli talk about Najee. I think she's in love...

CHAPTER THIRTY

"Everybody's been callin' me nigga
my whole damn life
pointin' and sayin' nigga til I think it's right
Hold my head up high
walk with all kinds of pride
but inside I be nigga, nigga, nigga til I die
Sex ain't all that's inside of me
there's more in life to be
but nigga, nigga, nigga keeps huantin' me
directin' me
sayin' what I should be
nigga, nigga, nigga til I die
Some kinda way I gotta stop this thing
determine in my head what I am today
Halt the madness of becoming a lie
Or. I'll be a nigga, nigga, nigga til I die...

for hours the music circulated aggressively throughout the moving vehicle, invading Tyress' being. Challenging him. Threatening him. Demanding that he define himself.

Who was he?

A rapist?

How had he allowed himself to come so close to hurting Niara-- his hands trembled a little as he gripped the steering wheel. His eyes focused on the road before him, but saw nothing. His mind was in a turmoil. This was not the life he wanted. This

221

was not the future for him. Deep down inside-- somewhere. He wanted more. To live. To hope. To dream. Instead of cruising the streets, waiting for the allure of danger to consume him...

He slowly released the steering wheel with his left hand and picked up the cell phone. With some difficulty, he dialed 729-2557.

One ring.

Two rings.

Three ring-- "Hello?"

He paused, "Niara."

Silence.

He continued, "Please do not hang up."

She wanted to, but something in his tone made her stop.

"Niara?" he repeated.

"Yes," she whispered.

"I know I hurt you."

She listened.

"I was wrong," he continued.

"You tried to rape me" she stated.

"I know," he said.

"But why?

"... I don't know," his voice sounded frustrated.

She waited for an answer. Some kind of explanation. Anything to make her understand what happened two weeks ago.

"I should not have treated you like that," he continued.

Niara heard her mother coming up the steps.

"Who's on the phone?" asked Cathleen.

She didn't answer.

"I'm leaving Philadelphia," he stated "I've got to get away.

Think about some things. If I stay here, it could get real ugly."

"I know," she said.

"I'm going someplace far. I want to start all over-- try to become the man I want to be-- should be. Goodbye," he said.

The telephone became quiet. She stared at it and felt hot tears run down her face. They wouldn't stop. They ran down the mouth of the phone and onto her hand, and onto the cord.

Her mother approached her quietly. As the older woman neared her daughter, she could see the tears. Some of her own pain returned to her. It hadn't been that long ago when she too had been hurt by Nathaniel. She gently reached out and stroked her daughter's cheek-- trying to wipe some of the pain away, " I know it hurts," Cathleen consoled softly. "But not forever."

NIARA

WHAT DO YOU THINK ABOUT THE BOOK?